Y0-BGG-947

Garfield County Libraries
Glenwood Springs Branch
815 Cooper Avenue
Glenwood Springs, CO 81601
(970) 945-5958 • Fax (970) 945-7723
www.GCPLD.org

Wolfsangel

Wolfsangel

John Reinhard Dizon

Chapter One

The skies were black at three o'clock that afternoon.

The hammer rose and fell with methodical precision, the dull thuds echoing throughout the dead silence of the snow-covered terrain. The cries of the victim filled the air as first his wrists, then his ankles, were nailed to the frosty wooden cross. Blood spurted and pooled freely across the ground, spattering the clothing of his grinning torturers.

Once the victim was secured, the cross was raised between those of his fellow captives. They writhed and groaned as their body weight caused unbearable pain to their impaled joints, and their lungs compressed from the distortion of their torsos. The soldiers laughed and taunted them, admiring their fiendish handiwork. One of the soldiers had nailed a sign on the cross over the head of the newly crucified victim. Upon it was a crudely etched *wolfsangel*[1], a medieval Germanic clan totem. It was the military symbol of the Kingdom[2].

"What are we going to do?" one of the victims' friends asked as they crouched behind a rock line in the distance.

"Carl is trying to circle them," his comrade replied. "It's our only chance."

"Can you hear me?" the leader of the squad surrounding the crucifixion scene stepped forth, calling into the darkness. "I know you're out there. You can put them out of their misery by coming out with your hands behind your head."

Another man came forth with a can of petrol in his hand. He handed it to the leader, who raised it aloft.

---

1. *wolf's hook*
2. Das Reich

"It is too cold out here!" the man bellowed. "We need a fire to warm us up! Either you come out and we can leave together to a warmer place, or we'll build a bonfire here!"

Carl Hanson heard the threats and moved as quickly as he dared. He was patrolling the area with two other fire teams when they came across a Red Army recon squad. They killed four of them in a crossfire but ran out of ammo in the ensuing shootout. Captain Ruess and his lieutenants were captured, stripped and beaten in the freezing Siberian temperatures. The Reds found lumber in the ruins of a nearby barn and created the monstrous spectacle on a nearby hill. Hanson had one grenade and four rounds left. He was sure it would be enough.

He crept up the side of a hill on his outstretched limbs like a giant spider, distributing his weight so as to avoid dislodging any rocks or debris. He had his rifle across his shoulders, his grenade in one hand and Mauser in the other. He crawled as far as he dared until his head was level with the ground upon which the torture took place. At once he was startled by a great burst of flames as the crucified soldiers were consumed by the ignited gasoline.

Carl sprung from his position, hurling his grenade into the midst of the soldiers. There was a great roar as the soldiers were scattered about, the crosses toppling atop them. Some reached for their weapons but Carl took them out with a shot to the head. His teammates rushed up the hill to his side, tending to their crucified comrades.

"Mongols," Sgt. Beckmann snorted as he tore the woolen cap off the partially severed head on one of the Reds, swatting at the ponytail at the base of the shorn skull. "We're seeing more and more of these devils."

"They spent their time killing each other before the war," Sgt. Garthaffner grimaced. "They would rape and kill the women in neighboring villages. The survivors' own people would leave the bastard offspring out for the wolves."

"Carl!" Sgt. Von Hoffman shouted. "Captain Ruess is still alive!"

"Poor bastard," Sgt. Tollner shook his head.

"Strip the Mongols and wrap him up," Carl ordered. "Make a pallet so we can get him out of here. Let's take the heads off these pieces of shit and bring them back as well. We'll let them know we're still the meanest sons of bitches in this valley."

The soldiers carried their woeful burdens over a kilometer back to the rendezvous point where they were loaded into a waiting truck and taken back to their base another kilometer away. They were screaming for medics, who rushed to take possession of the makeshift stretcher and move the burn victim to the emergency tent.

"What in hell happened, Hansen?" Major Wulf and Captain Kahn came to meet them.

"We ran directly into a squad of Red Army soldiers on patrol," Carl growled as his comrades removed the parcels containing the severed heads from sight. "They took Ruess, Slater and Dietz out and we didn't have enough ammo to push them back. Either we start getting enough ammo to fight out there or we're going to take a hell of a lot more casualties."

"You know our situation, Hansen," Wulf grumbled. "Our supply lines have literally been frozen shut out here. The trucks can't make it out this far. HQ has ordered that we ration the ammo out to a clip a man. Do you get anything off the Reds?"

"I wouldn't bring that garbage of theirs to a water gun fight," Carl scoffed. "No explosives, nothing of value. We found rat and squirrel meat in their rucksacks."

"Let's wipe the country clean of these bastards and get back home, Carl," Kahn patted him on the shoulder. "Stalingrad's just a shot away."

"If they don't do it to us first," Carl trudged away towards the bonfires lit around the camp, surrounded by freezing soldiers trying to stay alive.

The Third Reich unleashed Operation Barbarossa in declaring war on Russia in the Spring of 1941. The USSR, unable to cope with the blitzkrieg attack of the Luftwaffe and the Panzer tank divisions of the German Army, ceded hundreds of miles of territory in just a few short weeks. They had reached the outskirts of Stalingrad and were within reach of Moscow by autumn. Only the Russian winter arrived early, and the Siberian Express surged down from the Arctic Circle and froze the German Army in their tracks. The Germans found themselves dismally unprepared for the brutal winter. Hundreds of soldiers died of exposure in the subzero temperatures of the night. The Russians, who lived and worked in such an environment all their lives, were able to stem the tide of the German attack and were threatening to regain the ground they had lost just months before.

He was greeted by his joyful comrades as he approached the campfire, fueled by furniture salvaged from the shelled-out homes of Russian peasants in nearby villages. They gave him a bottle of vodka, and he was able to swallow an eighth of a liter in one mighty gulp.

"Here, Lieutenant," Eric Von Hoffman held out a bottle of barbiturates. "These will help you sleep."

"You get used to those, and they'll help you sleep forever," Carl retorted. "You'll get slow enough so even a Mongol can put a bullet in your head."

"I'll take my chances," Eric sniggered.

"I won't have any trouble getting to sleep, I've had my workout for the day. You'd better get some sleep, soldier, we're moving into that village down the road in the morning."

"I got a little more energy to burn, Lieutenant, but I'll be ready."

"Good," Carl walked off. "Ivan'll be waiting."

The Leader Regiment[3] 1st Platoon was on the move at daybreak, Carl leading his men in a pincer movement around the small village located two kilometers from the Waffen SS camp. Beckmann and Garthaffner led their men along the right flank as Tollner and Von Hoffman circled to the left. They took positions along the perimeter as 2nd Platoon approached slowly in a motorized convoy from the west. The soldiers huddled in the bitter morning cold, rifles at the ready as the village stirred at the sound of the oncoming vehicles.

The SS convoy slowed to a halt as they watched a group of older people converging in the middle of the small village. They watched through binoculars as groups of children came from their shacks bearing small parcels and baskets from which flowers protruded. They handed these to the women, who eventually began trudging through across the snowy ground towards the convoy.

"Damn it to hell," Major Wulf's voice crackled angrily across their radio sets. "What in hell will they think of next? Get one of our translators up there front and center. Tell those people to go back to their homes. If anyone sees glass or metal we open fire."

"I see glass, Major," a rifleman reported over the radio. "Looks like it may be wine bottles, they're in some of the baskets along with bread and cheese."

"How in hell do we know it's not those Molotov cocktails?" Wulf shouted back. "You get somebody out there who speaks barbarian and move those people back now!"

"The translator's on a motorbike, he's coming up from the rear, sir!" another voice broke in.

---

3. Der Fuehrer's

"The villagers are approaching the trucks, sir," a tank gunner reported. "They're at a hundred meters."

"Get someone on the speakers! Order them to halt!" Wulf yelled. "Lt. Hansen, ready to fire on my order!"

"Brains and gravy coming up," Eric chuckled in his position nearby Carl.

"Not one shot until I give the order," Carl warned him.

The biker and his passenger arrived at the front of the convoy, the translator scrambling clear as a rifleman gave him further instructions. The Siberian's eyes glazed over with fear as he numbly approached the group of peasants. He called out to them but they continued their wordless approach.

"Damn him!" Wulf barked. "Sergeant, get behind that dog and kick his ass forward or put him down!"

The biker got off his chopper and trotted up behind the translator, screaming orders as the man lurched forth. The greeting party grew nigh and, at length, began unwrapping their baskets and parcels to reveal the presents within.

"Ready! Aim!" Wulf's voice crackled.

"On my order," Carl shouted to his rifle squads.

At once, about a dozen of the shawled peasants sprang away from the group, brandishing automatic rifles that spat fire into the SS convoy. The translator's head exploded like a gourd, the biker behind him convulsed by rifle fire.

"There are men in the group!" Carl ordered. "Open fire!"

The SS riflemen unleashed a barrage of machine gun and rifle fire that tore the shacks in the tiny village asunder. They were somewhat surprised by the return fire and realized that a partisan unit must have staged the ambush. They were equally dismayed by the fact that women and children had been chosen to bait the feeble trap.

"Put a couple of cannon rounds into those houses, and see if we can get some air support," Wulf ordered. "Everyone stay covered until I give the word."

A Panzer tank rumbled out of the convoy and lazily positioned its turret in the direction of the village. The SS commandos watched as the tank seemed to dawdle before spitting a single shell at the tattered village. At once there was a deafening roar as an entire row of shacks exploded into flames and smoking rubble. A second roar took out the opposite side of the village directly in front of Carl's flank.

"Why in hell do they do that?" Tollner muttered. "Sacrificing women and children like that."

"We'll find a mass grave in those woods up ahead," Carl exhaled tautly. "The insurgents come to a town and demand that everyone help them fight the invaders. Anyone who refuses is condemned for treason against the State."

"You know, I hate to say it," Tollner said quietly as the commandos rose from their positions to investigate the charred ruins, "but there are a lot of people in the SS with that mentality."

"They're already doing it in the Occupied Territories," Carl growled. "They're recruiting able-bodied Slavs to work with the Einsatzgruppen units. Do you think those death squads following us around are all native Germans?"

"Death squads," Tollner spat into the snow. "It provokes things like this. We've gotten reports from interrogated prisoners that the countryside's full of horror stories about SS units gathering villagers and shooting them at mass graves. The way they look at it, they're going into the ground anyway, so why not die fighting?"

"Major," a voice crackled over the radio. "We've got women and children in the center of the village. We don't think anyone else survived, we'll check the houses once the flames die down."

"Tell your men to check for tunnels and trapdoors," Wulf's voice crackled. "Einsatzgruppen[4] on the way."

"You burn to death, and then you get to go to hell," Tollner shrugged.

"Just like Robert Ruess," Carl said quietly.

* * *

"What's the prognosis?" Carl asked as he slumped into a chair at Captain Kahn's desk in his spacious tent, thanking him for a cup of tea.

The regiment had proceeded another ten kilometers before it was decided that they would set up camp for the evening. The routine had become the most grueling part of the tour, setting up camp, tearing it down, and the ever-present concern that there were peasants ahead, to either kill or turn over to the Einsatzgruppen. It became a never-ending drudgery that only the bloodcurdling thrill of battle or the haze of alcohol abated.

"Grim," Kahn responded. "His face and chest were severely burned. It exhausted our resources just to keep him from dying of shock. We're trying to get him on a plane to Krakow but he refuses to go."

---

4. SS death squad

"What?"

"This is a hard situation," Kahn poured a shot of cognac, passing one over to Carl. "Ruess has family that's married into the Goerings. Apparently he had some calls made. He's calling in some big markers to remain on the field. His SS lawyer says there could be an investigation as to why his unit was ordered to retreat from their battle position."

"Investigation!" Carl thundered. "We told them to withdraw because they were surrounded by terrorists! They told me to retreat as well and if I had, we wouldn't be in this spot because this fellow would be toast!"

"We have to remember that he is in an extreme state of trauma right now," Kahn sipped his drink. "He's trying to turn himself into Captain Ahab and kill the Red whale. He's not going to be able to get back on the field and command troops for quite some time. Hopefully he will accept his situation and resign his commission before it creates a problem."

"You know he's been reckless bordering on suicidal out there. It's like following a pack of mad dogs. He's lost three lieutenants since we've been here. If he decides to stick to procedure and send his lieutenants without him, more men will die."

"Come now, Carl. Men will die regardless. This is war, and even worse, this is the Waffen SS. You trained under Eicke, you knew what you were getting into. Look, if this was a game of chess, you'd be a grandmaster. You're a legend, at your age. The reason why you're still alive is because of your wizardry on the field. Strategy, tactics, incredible skill, you've got it all. Unfortunately so did Ruess, but he thought he was invincible. The ways of God are great and terrible, and sometimes we learn our lessons in the most horrific ways, especially in this life we've chosen. Ruess is not accepting his lot, and all we can hope is that someone in authority will intercede before either he or his men suffer even greater loss."

"So he thinks he's going back out there," Carl exhaled tautly. "He's broken the rules, you know. He's brought witness against his comrades. No one outside his team will ever risk their lives for him again."

"No one can ever hear such words, Carl."

"I speak to you as a friend. I only ask that you do everything in your power to stop this lunacy."

"I'm meeting with the Colonel this evening. There is a very important directive from Berlin that will be addressed. Afterwards I will bring this concern to him directly."

"It's in God's hands, eh?

"God or the Devil?"

"Does it make a difference?"

"Not out here," Kahn shook his head ruefully.

The Leader Regiment began its slow withdrawal towards East Poland in the same direction from which they had come. It was easy to see where they had been welcomed by the civilian populace as liberators from Communist repression, and where the people rose up out of fear of rumored Nazi genocide. There were also some towns through which the regiment had passed peacefully but were now smoking ruins after acts of arson and murder by Red activists.

Colonel Stadler met with Majors Wulf, Diekmann, Kampfe and Weidinger the next morning to inform them of stunning developments on the Western front. He had gotten word that the Allied Expeditionary Forces had launched their invasion of Europe on the coast of Normandy just hours ago. OKW[5] had decided that they would recall the Kingdom Division from the Eastern Front and redeploy them to Normandy to repel the invasion force.

The news crackled through the division like electricity as the soldiers were ecstatic with joy. They were stationed in France just two years ago, and for those who remembered it was as paradise compared to the Russian wastelands. The trip across France would be as a mini vacation, regardless of the desperate battle ahead. Most of the soldiers of the division were fully confident that they would throw the invaders back into the sea.

It was late on the evening of June 4th, 1944 by the time the Leader Regiment reached their destination, about seventy kilometers from the Polish border. They estimated that they would reach the German border by June 5th, and would most likely cross into France by June 6th. They fully expected to engage in combat against the Allies by June 10th at the latest. The Division Commander, General Lammerding, instructed his colonels that his men were to relax and recuperate as best they could in preparation for the life-and-death struggle ahead.

Carl and his teammates had just the place in mind.

---

5. German Military Command

Sasha's Inn was a well-known bed and breakfast motel in a small village outside Uman where the proprietor, Sasha, had moved from Poland after leaving Germany shortly after the Kristallnacht pogrom in 1938. She was a beautiful Russian woman who had married a German Jew, and he sent her ahead to Krakow so he could consolidate his affairs. He was murdered by the SA during Kristallnacht but his brother-in-law was able to complete his dealings and send the money to Sasha. She fled to Russia after the German invasion and bought the bed and breakfast, which flourished as Polish Jews began migrating to Russia to escape the Nazis' efforts to address the Jewish problem. No one knew what to expect when the Germans invaded Russia, but they were delighted by Sasha's Inn and boarded its officers there in return for handsome compensation.

"Carl! Heinz!" the worried look on her face broke into joyous relief upon seeing her old customers at the door. "How wonderful it is to see you again!"

Heinz Barth was Carl's fellow lieutenant in the Company, and they had spent a memorable time at Sasha's during the Company's first trip through the village. As soon as they arrived in town they agreed to high-tail it to the inn.

"You're not closed, are you?" Heinz asked.

"Not for you," she smiled. "Come on in."

It was daybreak, and most of the regimental troops knew the drill in setting up camp and establishing their perimeters for the duration of their stay. SS riflemen chose the optimum positions in setting up sniper nests, as fire teams fortified checkpoints to monitor the flow of traffic in and around the village. Supply teams ran hoses down wells and merchants negotiated painfully with the soldiers, mindful of their responsibility to their neighbors not to sell out their stock to the detriment of the community.

"Where's Captain Ruess and his lieutenants?" she asked as they sat at the small bar in the parlor.

"We had an ugly scrape just down the road," Heinz ran his fingers through his shaggy blond mane. "Ruess was badly injured. The others didn't make it."

"How terrible," she murmured, fixing them glasses of wine and cognac, trying to absorb the shock of the news about Ruess. "Were you forced to retreat?"

"Actually we're on the way back to Poland," Carl thanked her for the wine. "They decided to give us a break. They felt that zero temperatures would be more tolerable than sub-zero."

"We're low on supplies right now," Sasha was apologetic. "Do you think...?"

"No problem," Carl snapped his radio from his belt.

Within minutes an SS rifleman brought a rucksack full of steaks, sausages and chicken. Sasha was profusely thankful and soon had a couple of steaks on the stove in the kitchen along with boiling potatoes and cabbage.

"Let's sit by the fireplace," she entreated them. "I so want to hear more about your studies in France while you were at the University at Gottingen, Carl. I find French art so fascinating."

"I think I'll need a double when you go back to the bar," Heinz rolled his eyes.

They chatted on into the day, pausing only to allow the officers to enjoy a sumptuous meal. After sunset, the two men decided to retire to their rooms as Captain Kahn arrived for dinner, bed and bath. The Waffen SS was notorious for its laxity regarding fraternization, yet the notion of lieutenants socializing with the captain could well be construed as favoritism in a different time and place in a highly competitive SS infrastructure.

"Nightcap?" Heinz held out his cognac bottle.

"I think I'd better get some rest," Carl decided. "Riding shotgun on a Panzer truck for twenty hours, and talking culture and politics with Sasha for six hours has just about done me in."

The commandos retired into their rooms and collapsed into a deep slumber. Only Carl was disturbed by a rustling below his window, and rolled out of bed to investigate without standing or turning on the lamp. He peered into the shadows below and perceived two figures darting through the bushes. He moved from the window and retrieved his rifle, slipping on his boots before crawling to the wall adjoining Heinz's room. He knocked quietly before crouching to the door and entering the corridor.

"Carl!" Heinz hissed as he emerged from his room brandishing his rifle.

"There's movement outside," Carl informed him. They tiptoed downstairs into the parlor where the fireplace continued to smolder. At once they saw Sasha coming into the room carrying an object in her arms. Carl was about to whisper to her when they saw Sgt. Beckmann creeping in through the front door. He aimed and fired, dropping Sasha and her burden to the carpet as chaos broke loose outside.

"She's the owner!" Carl thundered. "What did you do!"

"The captain had me posted on guard outside," Beckmann insisted. "The property's crawling with insurgents!"

"She was carrying a log for the fire!" Heinz snapped at him.

"What in hell's going on out here!" Kahn burst out from his room on the second floor.

"Hans, get him out of here! Move out the back, we'll distract them at the front door!" Carl ordered.

Kahn ran down the stairs and followed Beckmann to the rear exit. Carl and Heinz threw kitchen chairs through the curtained parlor windows, firing at the insurgents as the glass shattered across the cobbled garden outside. The rebels took up positions across the lawn and began returning rifle fire. The commandos began retreating towards the rear exit but stopped at the sound of breaking glass and the sudden bursts of flames throughout the motel.

"Molotov cocktails!" Heinz hissed.

"Not my favorite after-dinner choice," Carl growled.

They raced back upstairs and started for Carl's room but noticed the wisps of smoke and brightness coming from under the door. They opted for the bathroom and turned on the faucets but found that the water supply had been cut off.

"Cute," Carl smirked. "We'll have to go through the ceiling."

"And how do you propose to do that?"

"Bend over," Carl retorted. Heinz shook his head and braced himself against the sink as Carl pulled off his boots and hopped up on his back. Carl pulled out his bayonet knife and began hacking furiously at the ceiling. It began giving way under his manic assault, and soon plaster chips gave way to wooden splinters before Heinz could hear the breaking of the roof tiles above.

"Come on!" Carl jumped off his back. He boosted Heinz up, and Barth clambered through the hole before Carl pulled his boots back on and hurtled off the sink up in the aperture.

He was barely able to maintain his footing on the slanted roof before the insurgents below heard their boots on the tiles. Carl and Heinz began firing and saw a couple of shadowy figures drop lifeless in the bushes. As return fire began rattling the tile around them, they discarded their rifles in favor of their rapid-fire, high-powered Mausers. They spent agonized moments huddling by the chimney stack, exchanging fire with the insurgents before they heard shouted orders in German along with the approaching sound of vehicles.

"Saved by the cavalry," Carl exhaled.

"Not a minute too soon," Heinz gasped.

The commandos slid down the tiled roof and dropped onto the ground as their comrades rushed to meet them.

"Is the Captain okay?" Carl asked.

"Beckmann got him out just in time," a rifleman replied. "He was their prime target, they were ordered to assassinate any officers in the house. Apparently someone notified the Reds that Sasha had officers staying here the last time we came through."

"They didn't mention anything to her," Carl said ruefully. "She was killed carrying wood to the fire."

The reinforcement troops made short work of the insurgents, taking out most of them with machine gun fire and executing those who surrendered. Carl's face reflected his distaste as he reported to Captain Kahn at his command post.

"Thanks for saving my life, Carl," Kahn poured a shot of cognac at his table, which Carl declined.

"It didn't have to go down like that," Carl was adamant. "The woman was carrying a log to the fireplace. What did Beckmann think it was, a rocket launcher?"

"I gave Beckmann orders to shoot to kill if there were any problems," Kahn said flatly. "I know you were friendly with the woman. Accept my apology."

"Case closed. So what's with this take no prisoners thing? There are people living in this village looking out their windows. Don't you think they're going to tell the Mongols what they've seen? I thought we were incorporating these territories into the Reich, not killing everyone in sight like those jackals in the Einsatzgruppen. We're telling them that they have no choice but to fight to the death. I don't see that saving lives on our end."

"I don't dictate policy, Carl, I follow orders like we all do. Berlin ordered us to crush all resistance with no exceptions. I'm not in the Einsatzgruppen, I don't control them. I'd like to put all those murderous bastards under a tank and mash them flat. Unfortunately they're assigned to every Waffen SS division in the service. Do you think we're the only ones being followed by those scavengers?"

"We may not be able to stop them, but we don't have to be just like them."

"We're not, Carl," Kahn insisted. "We're not."

"I hope to hell things change when we go back to France," Carl turned to leave. "I hope to hell none of us have developed a taste for this."

"Things'll get a lot better," Kahn smiled, raising his glass. "*Vive la France.*"

"*Vive la France*," Carl grinned.

He was thinking about Angie.

Robert Ruess had graduated from the University of Hamburg in 1935, just four years before the outbreak of the war. He was torn between teaching science and accepting a job in research in the private sector, yet both were low-paying jobs by bourgeois standards in post-war Germany. He also had a dynamic spirit which yearned for something beyond the confines of the classroom and the laboratory, and considered a career in the military though the financial reward seemed just as dismal.

Magdalene Fock was a second niece of Baron Carl Fock, the father of Carin Fock, who was the first wife of Field Marshal Hermann Goering. She was a beautiful woman with flowing red hair, a statuesque figure, china blue eyes and a sensuous, full-lipped mouth. She and Ruess met during their junior year at the University, and it was a tempestuous relationship from the outset. She had hopes of one day ascending into Germany's upper class, and urged Ruess to join her vision quest in realizing her dreams.

After Goering had been appointed Interior Minister of Prussia, giving him full authority over the largest police force in Germany, the Nazi power play was in full swing. Goering incorporated the political and intelligence departments of the Prussian Police into his new organization, the Gestapo, which he placed under control of Heinrich Himmler. Himmler and his right-hand man, Reinhard Heydrich, were slowly developing their own elite force, the SS, into Adolf Hitler's Praetorian Guard. Himmler, already in control of all police forces outside Prussia, became the most powerful law enforcement official in Nazi Germany overnight.

The Nazis' hatred of Communism mirrored that of the Ruesses, who married shortly after graduation. It was Goering's meteoric rise that convinced the Ruesses to hitch their wagon to the swastika. Ruess first joined the SS, then took a position in forensics science with the Gestapo. He continually badgered Magdalene as he grew dissatisfied with his assignments, she in turn having him transferred via family connections to the SD[6]. Unknown to Magdalene, he had established contact with SS General Theodor Eicke, and enrolled in officer candidate training with the Waffen SS.

---

6. SS intelligence

Magdalene was furious but stuck by Ruess until he graduated and was assigned to the Kingdom Division at a respectable pay rate. Between their protracted battles over Ruess' failed attempts at breaking the glass ceiling restricting their social climb, the Ruesses were often seen at the finest social and cultural events in Hamburg and were continually recognized as a striking couple. They delighted in long walks along the Elbe near their home in Hamburg by day, and frequenting the City of Bridges' places of interest by night. The Deutsches Schauspielhaus[7], the Kunsthalle Hamburg Museum of Art and the Hamburg State Opera were among their favorite haunts. Magdalene often exchanged cards on holidays with her famous second cousin and alluded to those contacts with their acquaintances as they rubbed elbows when Ruess' schedule permitted.

Ruess was mindful of those better times when he strolled along the outskirts of Uman, a small town about fifty kilometers south of Kiev with Sasha, proprietress of her self-named cozy little inn. The Division was on its way across the Dnieper River into the Eastern Ukraine to suppress a series of terrorist attacks against the German Army and discovered Sasha's Inn, where Ruess, Captain Kahn and their lieutenants immediately sought lodging. Sasha made quick friends with Ruess, his lieutenants Dietz and Slater, as well as Carl Hansen and Heinz Barth, spending a merry evening of music, wine and cheese before the fireplace in the drawing room after dinner upon their arrival. Ruess and Sasha were the early risers on Sunday morning and decided on a stroll after tea.

"How long do you think the killings will go on after the war is over?" Sasha asked, her Nordic features striking in her natural environment.

"I don't think society condones killing outside of war," Ruess replied, his own ruggedly handsome features accentuated by his classic black officer's uniform and his heavy leather trenchcoat. "Unfortunately wars are not always recognized or declared."

"Such as the war against the Jews?" she lowered her eyes.

"The cause of war is not always what the combatants make it seem," he lit a cigarette and gave it to Sasha before lighting one for himself. "Almost every war since the beginning of time has been about economics, one side coveting the resources of the other. Race, religion and politics are purely semantic. Hitler feels that Communism is a ruse by the Jews to seize the assets of the working

---

7. German Theatre

class by taking control of the government. Many see this as a war against the Jews; I see it as a war against Communism. Once Marxism has been destroyed, the Jewish question will prove inconsequential."

They watched as a hawk swooped down in pursuit of a jackrabbit scampering frantically for the treeline ahead. As lightning, Ruess scooped up a handful of snow, packed a ball and fired it at the hawk, which flew away.

"How terrible is nature," she took his arm. "The rabbit lives so the hawk must starve."

"Yes," he patted her hand, "and so the German prospers at the expense of the Jew."

They walked arm in arm back to the inn, Ruess turning to her and touching her face before they entered.

"You're a beautiful woman, Sasha, with such a good heart and a wonderful personality," he smiled. "I am looking forward to returning and seeing you again. Remember, you will do well."

"Thank you, my friend," she reached up and kissed him. He next took her into his arms and gave her a long, passionate kiss before they headed back to reality.

"All right, fellows, here's the plan," Major Wulf met with his captains and lieutenants in the cottage they had requisitioned as a command post not far from Sasha's that evening. "We move out tomorrow and cross the Dnieper towards the eastern Ukraine border. Weather permitting, we should be able to set up camp before dark. What we're hoping to do is draw the terrorists in the region into a firefight and destroy their major units on the field. They're attacking our flanks in Central Russia and disrupting our supply lines, which is costing lives in this environment. Our objective is to clear the road for your battalion so you can secure the area for the Division to act as a rearguard and provide emergency backup for our Army Group in Russia."

"Otto and I have decided that the best strategy will be to set up a triple decker a few kilometers outside of camp," Ruess explained. "We'll run recon along the killing ground with Dietz's squad and set a trap with Slater's men. Here's the turn: the terrorists have been outflanking our backup units before overrunning our patrols. We think that if we set up a bracket with Carl, Heinz, Dietz and Slater, we can take them out. We'll use Carl and Heinz's squads to fill the brackets."

"Permission to leave our squads home and do our own work," Carl countered gruffly. "We're wasting men and material on jobs like this, not to mention the obvious problems with noise discipline. These people hunt jackrabbits out here to survive the winter, don't you think they'd make a bunch of SS men bouncing around in the snow in the dark? Plus you're rationing my ammo, I can't get more than a clip or two for these kinds of jobs. What'll you cut me down to after this Wild West shootout, six shots per trip?"

"All right, then bring your sergeants along," Ruess conceded.

"Carl will lead his unit, I'll take Dietz and Slater."

"Why are you going if Otto stays home?" Carl asked, creating a murmur among the others in the room.

"Do you have a problem with my organizational skills, young Captain?"

"The problem," Carl insisted, "is your Errol Flynn escapades out there. You go offsides too often and it forces me to play my hand too early. Permission to run my pattern with Heinz, I'll send Eric, Hans, Michael and Peter to backup Dietz, Slater and their sergeants, if you insist on so many men."

"Permission denied," Ruess lit a cigarette impatiently. "We need the force of numbers, we don't know how many terrorists are hitting us. We'll be harvesting their supplies, Ivan's on his home field, there should be plenty to go around. Plus, we're recon. If we've got a bunch of water buffaloes out there who can't make it on the snow, perhaps they'll be more suited on the front lines with the regular Army, or in the rear with the gear and the death squads."

"I always thought he looked more like Clark Gable than Errol Flynn," Wulf smiled as the others joined in laughter. "Point taken, but I'll have to side with Ruess. You take quite a few chances yourself out there, Carl, and I'd rather use up all our ammo than lose a few good men."

"Fine," Carl conceded. "I hope the entire ensemble comes back in one piece."

Ruess remembered little to nothing after the ambush, heavily medicated until he had stabilized. When informed of his prognosis, he immediately implemented a previously-conceived plan in having his SS lawyer contacted. He asked that all proceedings on his behalf be placed on hold until he was in full command of the situation. Having done so, he called the chief doctor to his room for a briefing.

"You've suffered extensive tissue damage to your face and chest," Dr. Stein reported. "There may also be muscle, tendon and nerve damage as well. I'm having you sent back to Krakow for therapy before we get you back to Berlin for cosmetic surgery. We'll also be assigning you to a psychologist for counseling and therapy during the rehabilitation process."

"So what's the damage?" Ruess asked. "Let's get the bandages off and let me have a look."

"Sir," Stein cleared his throat, "I don't think it's fair to you or us to remove the bandages this early."

"I need to know where I stand. It's my future we're talking about here. Let's just say you're doing an early bandage change."

The doctor grudgingly produced a pair of scissors along with fresh gauze, padding and ointment. He dutifully cut through Ruess' bandages and located a mirror which he silently handed over.

"Holy shit," Ruess managed. "I'm seriously fucked up."

"Miracles have been known to occur in this day and age," Stein cleared his throat. "With the new technology we have available, skin grafting is becoming less of a phenomenal procedure. Plus, our SS doctors in field research facilities such as Auschwitz are making remarkable breakthroughs in treating battlefield injuries…"

"Tape me back up and get my SS lawyer in here," Ruess said menacingly.

Hours later, Lieutenant Franken of the SS Legal Department arrived and was escorted to the local hospital in Kiev that had been requisitioned by the Regiment. He found Ruess in an armchair staring pensively out the window.

"Dr. Stein says you are refusing painkillers," Franken took a seat in a flimsy armchair across from Ruess in the spartan room.

"I need my mind sharp," Ruess replied. "You know, I always considered the fact that you could lose an arm or a leg out here. I never thought about losing my face, but that could be a blessing in disguise. You can't go back on the field missing a limb, but, given this, I can get back out there and fix those Commie bastards."

"Captain, you've given enough to the Fatherland. It's time to go home now."

"Let me tell you something," Ruess turned to stare at him. "My wife and I used to lie around and fuck all day when I went home. Any idiot can see those days are over. First, I want you to make sure that I get back on the critical list, and I don't come off until I say so. Next, I want out of here. I want to be sent along with the gear over to our staging area in France. I need comfortable quarters and absolute privacy. I'm going to continue operating on the field but I need to do so independently of the Division. I'm not going to let a bunch of paperwork stop me from wiping Communism right off the map."

"I'm not sure how we're going to go about that, sir."

"ODESSA," Ruess grinned malevolently. "You put me in touch with ODESSA."

"I…don't believe such an organization actually exists, Captain…"

"Let's look at it this way. My wife gets cards from Carin Goering on every Church holiday. If I told her that my career was going to be shipwrecked because my lawyer was being uncooperative, I think she'd be screaming for your head on a pike. You know Goering gave Himmler the power, he's still got the leverage, why gamble against it? Stay on my side, I'll make sure that when the time comes, they draw a line under your name instead of through it."

"I'll do all in my power," Franken said as he took his leave.

Ruess chuckled quietly as he watched the door close behind Franken.

The time for drawing lines, he decided, had come to an end.

Chapter Two

The summer of 1939 was an idyllic time in France.

Despite the rumors of war, everyone was certain that the politicians would prevail in the midnight hour. Hitler was bluffing, it was said, and he had achieved all his goals in restoring Germany as a major power in post-war Europe. The British had been pushed to their limit and agreed that they would join France in crushing any acts of aggression by the Nazis. Students in both France and Germany agreed that war was not the answer, and the younger generation would do their utmost in convincing their parents not to repeat the tragic mistakes of the last decade.

Angelique Dagineau had known Carl Hansen since their freshman year at Gottingen University. They began dating in their sophomore year, were an item on campus as juniors, and made commitments to one another as seniors. Only Carl had enlisted at graduation and sought to hedge his bets by enrolling in an elite German unit to avoid assignment to the dreaded trenches of the previous war. He was sent to boot camp in August, and it was not until the Christmas holiday before he was able to take leave and visit her at her home.

Her father Francois was the mayor of their hometown and considered one of the most influential men in their province. The Dagineau vineyards were among the most reputable in southern France, and their wines considered among the best in the country given a favorable harvest. Francois was a true patriot who served in the war and was devastated by the Nazi invasion. He devoted himself to protecting and defending his community, working diligently with the Nazis and the Vichy government to those ends. Yet he lived for the liberation of his nation and would do anything he could to realize that dream.

She was his only child, and when her mother died during Angie's childhood, father and daughter were left alone. She grew to be a beautiful Frenchwoman, with flowing auburn hair, violet eyes, ruby lips, a proud bosom and an athletic figure. He doted on her but never allowed her to lose her Christian humility, and demanded her best throughout her scholastic years. When she introduced him to Carl, Francois was joyous in knowing that she had made an excellent choice in the debonair, sophisticated and respectful young man.

She would never forget the pain and indignation in her father's eyes when Carl arrived at their chateau dressed in the black and silver uniform of the SS. The realization in Carl's face of its effect on her father was just as devastating. Her father made an excuse of being summoned by the Nazis, ordering the servants to spare nothing in making Carl and Angie's reunion a joyous occasion. Regardless, Francois and Carl never met again, and Francoise would speak of him no more.

They continued to correspond, even after Carl's division was deployed to Russia in support of the new campaign. They exchanged romantic letters, sent pictures and keepsakes, keeping their love alive for five long years. Now, at last, it was the Carl was in France, and he arranged to see her.

At long last.

Angie negotiated her way through the dusty streets of Montauban, its cobblestones and dirt roads torn asunder by the tank treads of the motorized units. She was alarmed by the appearance of the tall, lean, muscular commandos in their T-shirts, camouflaged pants and combat boots. Weapons hung loosely from their shoulders and belts, and bandanas and sunglasses were common accessories. Many wore tattoos and most bore the scars of the field. They paraded around like brigands, and the women flocked around them like movie stars. They smoked and drank heavily, and the air was filled with raucous laughter and the shouts and yells of rowdy fighters.

"Excuse me, Mademoiselle."

Angelique whirled in the direction of the voice and found herself face-to-face with four heavily armed commandos.

"I apologize, but I must ask that you come with us."

"Of. . . of course."

Angie's stomach was knotted with trepidation as the commandos formed a bracket around her. She had heard all the horror stories about the inhuman carnage in Russia and the midnight raids of the Vichy police under directions of the Gestapo. She wore a pretty flowered summer dress and raised sandals, prettying herself for Carl. She prayed desperately that it would not entice these men into heinous action.

They led her down an alley, and her heart pounded like a jackhammer as her eyes sought desperately for whatever waited beyond. They strode silently alongside her, and she shuddered in relief as it brought them at length to yet another bustling street.

"Sir?" one of the men approached a comrade. "There is a person of interest you should be aware of."

The soldier turned to face them, and she nearly dropped her purse as her legs weakened.

"*Angie!*"

Carl was overwhelmed as she jumped into his arms. They hugged each other for an eternity before Carl felt a pat on the shoulder, noticing that the commandoes were sauntering away.

"You know what you are, don't you?" Carl growled after them.

"Loyal soldiers of the Reich, sir," one chuckled back.

"Here's something to enjoy the afternoon with," the soldier behind him handed him a bottle of wine. "This costs one hundred francs. If you don't like it, I'll kill the innkeeper."

"Nice," Carl showed the bottle to Angie.

"I'm sure," she smiled. "It's one of my father's."

"I can't believe you're here," he gazed into her eyes.

"Carl, what is this?" she was anxious. "I've seen the German Army in Paris, it is nothing like this. Is this...some kind of gang?"

"They have us on special assignment," he reassured her. "We get special privileges."

"And these...these scars. You never mentioned anything like this in your letters."

"This is why God has sent me an angel. He has already put me through Hell."

"Your...your arms, your chest, your shoulders. You look like a wrestler," she touched his bicep.

"It was so cold that we lifted weights constantly to keep from freezing to death," he smiled softly. "Come, let's get a basket and a blanket and enjoy the rest of the afternoon."

The couple sauntered into a nearby winery where the proprietor was quick to fill a picnic basket with a large piece of Brie, a large pate de foie gras and a loaf of freshly-baked bread. Carl also paid extra for one of the tablecloths, and soon the couple was on their way to the countryside.

They spread the cloth upon the grass as Carl pried open the wine bottle. Only they were overcome with emotion and fell into each others' arms in an everlasting kiss. It was as if heaven had burst through the clouds in a blaze of starlight, sending a legion of angels down as a glass bolt of lightning to swirl them out into the stratosphere, beyond the moon, through the planets, into an indescribable euphoric eternity that knew no limits, no beginning or ending, just pure and blissful glory...

"This is it, you know," he kissed her fingertips as they gazed at each other, contemplating the sheer beauty they fathomed in each others' eyes, "the final battle. If we toss them back into the sea they will have exhausted their re-sources, they won't be able to try it again. Plus it'll give us time to develop the new superweapon, far more devastating than the V-2 rocket. Yet, if they force their way in... with the barbarians at the eastern gates, all may be lost."

"It will be over, one way or another," she reached up and caressed his face. "We'll be together forever, nothing will ever separate us again."

"Where will you go now, after you leave?"

"Back to my father's house, to wait for you."

They embraced again and continued to kiss each other, intermittently stop-ping briefly to sample the food and wine they had brought, though it could scarce quench the hunger and thirst they had for each other. It was almost as if they had been given a reprieve from death itself, so urgent and insatiable was their desire. They managed to fill the void of five years with an afternoon of passion, and returned to town that late afternoon walking on air, their spirits soaring as doves.

As they came into town, Carl and Angie approached the medical trucks on their way back to the German border. They were both unsettled by the seem-ingly endless flow of trucks returning with soldiers injured on the beach at Normandy. Trucks filled with the dead seemed to outnumber the ambulances.

"It's a mess," one soldier moaned, his head entirely bandaged and one eye covered by gauze. "I've never seen so many ships in my life. They just keep com-ing and coming. The beaches are covered with dead, the wounded are falling atop each other. Yet they keep coming. It's almost as if they found a way to bridge the Atlantic."

"Carl," she touched his arm as they walked away from the medical convoy. "I'm so afraid."

"Don't be," he took her in his arms. "I just came back from Russia. I've lived through ice storms, sub-zero temperatures, terrorist attacks, air and artillery strikes, Mongol raids, you name it. Do you think that God would take me out right when I've gotten my darling Angie back after five years?"

"You know my father has connections with the *maquis*," she lowered her voice. "They have been working with the British for months preparing for this. As we speak they are holding political discussions with the underground that will lead to a major financing operation. They may be investing over a million francs in arming the Resistance. It's not just peasants with rifles and shotguns anymore."

"Make sure," Carl cleared his throat, "that you and Francois never speak a word of this to anyone. Promise me."

She wrapped her arms around his neck and they kissed each other as if for the last time. At length they reluctantly released each other, and there were tears in both their eyes.

"After this is over," he swore, "I'll come back to you."

"I believe you, my love."

They kissed once more before he walked her to the railroad platform, and after a lingering goodbye kiss, she was gone.

"I quote from a directive issued to both the 66th Reserve Corps and the Kingdom Division yesterday from OKW after the terror attacks at Groslejac, Cressenac and Noailles. 'Pass to the counteroffensive and strike with the utmost vigor and power, without hesitation. It is necessary to break the spirit of the population by making examples. It is essential to deprive them of all will to resist the *maquis* and meet their needs,'" the SS officer addressed the group in the room before he was interrupted by a new arrival at the door.

"Lieutenant Hansen. We've been waiting for you."

Carl arrived at the small home near downtown Toulouse that had been confiscated by the police from a known insurgent for use by the SS. He saw that Kahn, Barth and the platoon sergeants were in attendance. They were drinking and lazing around, playing cards, polishing weapons, a noticeable tension permeating the air.

"I had a personal matter to attend to," Carl replied, loosing his rifle from his shoulder and propping it against a wall. "You should've started without me."

"I am Lieutenant Gunter Schweinberg of the SD[1]," he introduced himself. He was a man of average build with slicked-back blond hair, cold blue eyes and an arrogant smile. His black uniform was meticulous and everyone made him for a prototypical SS fanatic. "I have been sent here under direct orders from General Kaltenbrunner to oversee and supervise the work of our Einsatzgruppen units assigned to the Leader Brigade. I am also under orders to ensure that all those in leadership positions have a clear understanding of our objectives in dealing with the insurgency problem here in France. Understandably, we were unable to start without you. Let me counsel you that this should not happen again."

Carl fought a murderous impulse yet managed to hold his tongue, instead exchanging glances with Kahn as the room filled with hums, whistles and mooing sounds.

"Uh...you said your name was Gunter?" Carl exhaled tautly.

"Lieutenant Schweinberg," he corrected Carl.

"Gunter," Carl cleared his throat. "Perhaps I should go back outside and come back in so we can start all over. Or maybe I should go back to whence I came and we'll wake up tomorrow like this never happened."

"Captain Kahn," Schweinberg turned to him, "I am well aware and, in fact, was duly briefed on the nature of the spirit of camaraderie that prevails among the ranks of the Waffen SS. I was instructed not to infringe upon the privilege that it entails. However, rest assured that my position as a representative of General Kaltenbrunner and, above and beyond that, Reichsfuhrer Himmler, supercedes any concerns for your team spirit. It would be unfortunate if I had to include this incident in my report."

"Suppose I told you to go fuck yourself? Would that be something to include in that report?"

Schweinberg whirled irately in the direction of the voice. He found himself locked in the cold-blooded stare of Eric Von Hoffman, the red-haired, blue eyed rifleman's gaze as emotionless as a killer shark. There was something in the look that drained him of his confidence as Eric blew a stream of smoke in his direction.

"Captain Kahn," Schweinberg turned to him. "A word in private, please."

---

1. SS Intelligence

"Now that's not polite," Eric flicked his cigarette just centimeters from Schweinberg's boot. "I'm talking to you."

"What is your name?" Schweinberg asked quietly.

"This isn't about the games you hot shots play in your fancy uniforms in your fancy offices in those fancy buildings back in Berlin," Eric stood up from his chair facing backwards towards the room. "This is a game of life and death out here."

"Eric," Kahn warned him.

"You know something?" Eric drew his pistol. "I got a game for you."

"Shit," Hans Beckmann lowered and shook his head

"Eric," Carl spoke up.

Hoffman jacked open the revolver and dumped the bullets onto the floor, keeping one pistol in his hand. He loaded in into a chamber, spun the loader and snapped it back in place, pointing it at Schweinberg's head.

"Are you mad?" Schweinberg gasped.

"No, not at all," Eric grinned devilishly. "Matter of fact, I'm happy as a clown. See how I'm smiling.

"Eric!" Kahn demanded.

"Too late, Captain," Eric replied, pulling the trigger. There was a deathly silence as the loud click of the hammer filled the room. Schweinberg recoiled as if punched in the stomach.

"You won," Eric marveled. "Let's go two out of three."

"Please!" Schweinberg dropped to his knees, shielding his face. "No more, for God's sake, no more!"

"Eric," Carl came up behind him and entwined his hand around his, interlocking his finger in the trigger guard. "Use your brains for once. We've got no one to tend this place for us. We'd have to bring in one of the frog women to clean up the mess. Do you know what kind of a mess this makes? A frog woman would walk in here and vomit. We'd have to toss her out, and then what would we have? Brains and blood all over the walls, and vomit all over the floor. I'm not hanging out in a place like that, Eric. So you find us another hangout place or keep this one clean in the meantime."

"Okay. Lieutenant, copy that," Eric smiled wickedly, turning to Schweinberg. "Well, you piece of shit, it looks like you live to see another day. Let me tell you something, though, it's not over. I've killed over thirty people in this war, men, women and children. I know when it's over they're not going to let me go home, ever again. I got nothing to lose by killing you. If I thought there was the slightest chance that I could get out of here by killing you, well, Carl could clean up the mess himself for all I care."

"All right, it's over. Please," Schweinberg begged.

"I'll find you, and I'll kill you," Eric said as Carl released his grip on the pistol.

"I understand," Schweinberg's voice quavered.

At once Eric pointed the gun at Schweinberg's head and pulled the trigger. Another loud click electrified the room as Schweinberg let loose a wailing cry. There was a second click as Carl cocked his gun and pointed it at Eric's head.

"That's enough, you crazy bastard," Carl warned him.

"You know, Carl," Eric smirked at him, slowly holstering his gun, "I always said that when it was my time, I was going to decide how it would go down. I'm not going to let you be the one. Somebody else, but not you."

"That really hurts, Eric," Carl snarled, uncocking and holstering the weapon.

"Both of you, get the fuck out of here," Kahn ordered. "You men, help the lieutenant up and fix him a drink."

"I think he pissed his pants," Barth murmured as Carl and Eric passed him by.

"Buy you a drink, Lieutenant?" Eric asked as they walked out the door.

"You get the second round," Carl slammed the door behind them.

* * *

"Thank you for saving my life, Lieutenant."

"I've been getting that more and more often."

"What is that man's story…Carl?" Gunter Schweinberg asked plaintively. He was dressed in a hound's tooth blazer, a yellow shirt and khaki pants, wearing his curly blond hair without the grease. "For my edification."

"For your edification," Carl exhaled. They were in front of a general store not far from the barracks the next day. Carl was passing by and Gunter caught his attention, as if he was loitering about but fearing to trespass.

"Eric's father was a Catholic priest who joined a monastery to avoid prison time. He was excommunicated for, shall we say, deviant sexual activity, and got married so he could have a wife and children to take it out on. His excuse was that since he was a priest, he represented God on earth and was, in fact, a son of God, like Jesus. Sometimes I think Eric believes he's carrying on in his father's footsteps."

"Has he ever been examined?" Gunter asked softly.

"They would have transferred him to the back of the pack with the Einsatzgruppen if he wasn't such a skilled commando," Carl grunted. "He's one of my best men. They've got a dossier on him in Berlin as big as an encyclopedia. He knows they'll never let him go. Once the war is over, they'll lock him up for the rest of his life."

"I'm just doing my job," Gunter pleaded. "I don't want to get killed down here."

"Quid pro quo," Carl shot back. "You watch my back, I'll watch yours. There's a lot of back-biting, dirty politics, illegal activity, you name it, out here. I may end up having to get my hands dirty to deal with it. I'll make sure everyone stays off your ass, including Eric. You just be ready to return the favor."

"Sure, Carl," Gunter replied eagerly. "You got a deal."

"Just one more thing."

"Sure, what's that?"

"Don't be an asshole."

"You got it, Carl," Gunter beamed.

Carl returned to his motel room only to find a note at the reception desk summoning him to Captain Kahn's quarters. He was slightly irked and figured he was going to get bitched out for the episode with Eric last night.

"Sir," Carl pushed open the door as it had been left ajar for the convenience of the staff.

"Have a seat, close the door," Kahn took off his glasses, seated at a small desk he had rearranged to face the entrance. "I understand you made the peace with Schweinberg."

"We're a happy family again," Carl nodded.

"Good," Kahn frowned. "I just got word that the Einsatzgruppen unit assigned to the Division has been redeployed to the Russian front. Berlin has given Schweinberg orders to oversee our counterinsurgency efforts. They've left a platoon behind for support. They've been given authority to recruit the local Gestapo forces if they need backup."

"So they've finally figured out a way to do things more efficiently for once."

"Apparently. The reason I called you over is to give you a heads up on our Ruess situation."

"So he's finally going in for treatment?"

"Not quite. The Colonel decided that since his unit was so depleted, he was going to disband it and reassign the men to Barth's company. They've got a couple of errands for you to run, so we'll be expecting Barth to pick up the slack while you're up and about. They may be assigning some of your men as the need arises, but it'll only be temporary at best."

"So has Ruess been decommissioned?"

"Actually, I sent a special request to Berlin to have him called in. The request was denied without explanation. Next, I was informed by Lammerding through Stadler that Ruess was being reassigned to command the Einsatzgruppen platoon."

"Now that's an unexpected twist," Carl smirked. "What does Schweinberg have on it?"

"Technically, that puts him under Ruess," Kahn shrugged. "Here's a better one. We found out our surplus gear has been scheduled for shipment to Limoges. We had one of our clerks do some research and we found out it's going to a chalet that was rented out by Berlin in Ruess' name."

"That tells me that now Ruess is under some sort of clandestine assignment," Carl speculated.

"To do what?" Kahn growled. "I go to Wulf and he gets stonewalled by Diekmann and Kampfe. Same old crap, the two of them against Wulf and Weidinger sitting on his thumbs doing nothing."

"What can you do," Carl threw out a hand. "The usual Division politics."

"The problem we have is that these frogs out here think the Second Coming is going on over in Normandy. It's approaching a state of hysteria. We need to get out there as quickly and surreptitiously as possible. We can't afford to stir up the hornets' nests out here. I think that's probably why they recalled the main Einsatzgruppen unit. Plus the fact that if we need Gestapo backup it works both ways, it gives them a show of force that keeps the terrorists in check."

"So you think Robert may be plotting his revenge against Communism by carrying out some kind of counter-terrorist action against the civilians out here."

"I'm not sure, but I know we can't afford it. We need to get to Normandy as soon as possible and in one piece, not detaching units to go chasing frogs all over the countryside."

"You think I should talk to him?"

"We've got something else in mind," Kahn tossed a dossier over to him. "We got word that the FFI[2] have a major conference scheduled in the Limousin region this evening. According to our sources, the Communist insurgent network has a series of attacks planned on government installations in this same region within the next forty-eight hours. We have reason to believe that the British SOE[3] may be working with the terrorists."

"I hear the FFI is a rival socialist group," Carl mused.

"Exactly," Kahn agreed. "This is why we want to keep them out of the game. We think we have a fix on the location of the scheduled meeting. It's a farm property in the middle of a small valley that affords the terrorists a commanding field position against a sizeable force. However, we think that one man with the necessary skills may be able to move in and destroy the target."

"I'm not sure if I should be so glad that my superiors have such confidence in my skills," Carl scowled.

"Ruess is gone and Eric probably wouldn't make it back. I wouldn't ask anyone else."

"I'm going to get a couple hours' sleep before I head out," Carl swiped the dossier off the desk. "I'll be sleeping in late in the morning, so don't even think of calling."

"Not unless the Americans show up," Kahn smiled back.

Hours later, Carl Hansen crept through the tall grass of the open field for nearly a quarter kilometer from the treeline. There was a silvery moon that was fleetingly shaded by cloud formations at intervals, allowing Carl the luxury of moving more quickly in the shadows. He saw no guards save for one at the doorway, indicating that the insurgents felt certain that the open field around the farmhouse provided its own security. He could see lights and movement, and as he drew nigh he could see the shadows and shapes of vehicles on the other side of the house. The man at the door held a submachine gun, indicating that this most likely was more than a meeting of the shotgun-toting *maquis*.

"Four million francs!" a voice thundered from inside the house as Carl could hear them bickering in French. "Who would be stupid enough to believe such a thing!"

---

2. French Forces of the Interior
3. Special Operations executive

"It came to us from a man who is near to De Gaulle's inner circle," another voice insisted. "Let's reason together. The British and the Americans are risking everything on the Normandy coast. Suppose the Nazis managed to repel the invasion. Both countries would be militarily bankrupt. Do you think four million francs would be a foolish investment, after all they've already wagered?"

"Let's not forget the rumors coming from America," a third man spoke up. "The American government is perceiving communism as the next great threat to democracy. Once they've defeated the Axis powers, they will be focusing on the Russians. What makes you think they will be anxious to support a communist government in France?"

"There is a very thin line between socialism and communism," yet another man retorted, "very little difference between the Hitlerites and the Stalinists. Do you think they will see us much differently than the FTP? Let me assure you, the Americans are a people of action, much more so than any other in history. They respect action and violence, it is part of their heritage, look at their Revolution, their Indian Wars, their Wild West, their Civil War. If we continue to show them that the FFI is a more dynamic force than the FTP, they will put their money on us. I guarantee that."

"How will the capitalists put money on you if there's no one around to collect?"

The twelve men seated around the table in the parlor were astonished by the voice they did not recognize. They whirled and saw their door guard dangling from a bayonet sticking out of his throat, eyes staring lifelessly at them. They began sprawling away from the table as the man holding the guard tossed his corpse aside and opened fire.

The first shotgun blast tore the head off the man at the head of the table, splattering it like an overripe melon. The next two shots hit the closest men to him in the back, hurling them across the floor. He then shot two men attempting to draw their weapons, ripping their faces from their skulls. He then dropped the shotgun and drew his Mauser, leaping onto the table and shooting every last man in the head.

Satisfied that everyone was dead, he walked around the room and ripped the pockets off their trousers, collecting wallets and tossing them on the table next to the maps and books in its center. He next shoveled them off into a large valise by the table, sealed it tight and vacated the farmhouse. As an afterthought, he unhooked the kerosene lamp from its place by the doorframe and tossed it back into the room. The building was soon engulfed in flames as Carl vanished into the darkness.

* * *

This is excellent, Carl," Colonel Stadler rocked back in his swivel chair at the center of the long table before which Carl stood. "Excellent work."

"He's the best," Major Wulf said proudly. "That nobody can deny."

The commanding officers of the Regiment sorted through the documents and made a sketchy outline on a chalkboard attempting to diagram the insurgents' initiatives. After a lengthy discussion they came to a general consensus.

"It doesn't make it any less of a problem," Major Diekmann frowned. "All it does is confirm our worst fears. Brive, Tulle, Limoges, Oradour. This is a hotbed of insurgent activity. I don't see any choice but to divide our forces and move in a pincer formation through the Limousin region in order to contain the rebel forces as we make our appointment in Normandy."

"I agree," Major Kampfe nodded. The two majors had served together in WWI and enjoyed a close friendship that gave them considerable leverage within the Regiment though they were careful not to overstep their bounds before the Colonel. "If we move directly towards the theatre of operations, we'll be running a gauntlet that will serve no purpose other than to entice these bandits."

"There is always an inherent risk in splitting our force," Major Weidinger ventured. He was the most prudent of the group, playing devil's advocate where possible to afford all sides a clearer view of the argument. He was also regarded with reservation by the others due to his background as a concentration camp guard at Dachau and Belsen. "Yet, of course, presenting a target also invites the enemy to err on the side of better judgment. Still, we cannot afford ourselves the luxury of indulging in these soft targets with such a prodigious task ahead of us."

"Carl," Stadler beseeched him. "Pull up a chair. You've come and gone on the field more than any other. Tell us what you think."

Carl pulled up a seat, mindful of the fact that he was encroaching on the territory of his superiors. Yet he knew the esteem he had earned among them and would give place to them when and if necessary.

"Give me minimal air and artillery support and I can move into Tulle, Limoges and Oradour and get things under control before the main forces arrive,"

Carl suggested. "We need the element of surprise on our side if we're planning to catch anyone in the act and get some good information. These terrorists are like gypsies, they perform their routine and then go into the wind. The sound of a convoy is an evacuation signal for these people. They won't stand and fight, we're foolish to expect such a thing. If you let me take my platoon in on foot we can cripple the terrorists and block their escape."

"Carl, the GMR[4] has informants in Paris who indicated the FTP has over 200 terrorists in Limousin, and the *Milice* [5] tells us there may be as many as 2,000 hardcore and associate members of the *maquis* in the region," Major Wulf pointed out. "We have no idea how many of them are stationed in or around Tulle, or Limoges or Oradour, for that matter. These people are invisible to the naked eye, they travel as civilians, you can't tell them until they're firing at you, we've gone through this in Russia, for heaven's sake."

"You're too damned valuable, that's what they're trying to tell you, Carl," Major Kampfe chuckled, having had a few drinks despite the early hour of the morning. "If there were a dozen more like you, you'd be off in a heartbeat. Unfortunately, the only one else is Von Hoffman, that psycho. Ruess is on his way to the loony bin, and Slater and Dietz are six feet under. You're our secret weapon, you can't be spared."

"In so many words," Major Diekmann cushioned his friend's diatribe.

"So they light a fire under the town and we have to blow it up at the cost of countless civilian casualties," Carl shot back. "It'll create a wave of hysteria throughout the region and cause more people to join the fight against us. We'll have to fight that much harder in Limoges and Oradour because of it. Colonel, I can move into Tulle with a handful of men, take out the terrorists and save lives."

"I don't see it happening without you losing at least half your squad in the process," Stadler decided. "Our recon units have been decimated since our tour of Russia and the replacements we're getting don't know their asses from their elbows about recon. I need your Company in one piece when we hit that shitstorm in Normandy, Carl, it's already making Kursk look like a snowball fight in comparison. We move in together, you work the point, if you have any problems we'll be right behind you."

---

4. *Groupes Mobiles de Reserve*, or Reserve Mobile Groups
5. Vichy militia

The *maquis* coordinated their attack that next morning on the village of Tulle on June 7, 1944. They had grudgingly joined forces with the FTP, [6], a Communist insurgent group with over 25,000 members on the streets of Paris. The FTP leader in Paris, Gilles Guevremont, sent a company of 100 men to the Limousin region for the combined assault against the 3rd Battalion/95th Security Regiment of the German Army manning the local garrison.

The overwhelmed garrison troops fought valiantly but were overwhelmed by the strength of numbers and were forced to surrender. The *maquis* stood aside once the converted schoolhouse was taken and watched in disgust as the Communists took hold of the captive soldiers and dragged them into the town square. They were beaten to death by the FTP cadre amidst the cheers and encouragement of the villagers, after which the bodies were mutilated and dragged back to the schoolhouse. Twenty-four other German soldiers on assignment in Tulle were also murdered by the FTP, raising the total to sixty-four deaths.

The FTP used the occasion to gain the support of the villagers for their cause. Their propaganda chiefs distributed literature and delivered speeches with bullhorns from balconies, stepladders and soapboxes. They promised that, upon the annihilation of the Nazi Empire by the advancing Red Army, the Russians would continue westward into France and secure a lasting peace with a benign Communist government led by the FTP. Never again would France live in the shadow of imperialist enemies, with the Anglo-Americans removed from the Continent and a benevolent USSR protecting its Eastern borders once and forever.

The *maquis*, along with the large number of WWI veterans who fought under General Petain, rolled their eyes and endured the rhetoric while reveling in their newfound freedom, no matter how fleeting it might be. The underground network broadcast, Radio Bastille, was delivering hourly blow-by-blow updates on the cataclysmic battle on the beaches of Normandy, and it seemed to be a matter of time before the Allied Expeditionary Force would release them from bondage...

...without the help of the USSR.

The city of Paris itself had become a cauldron of corruption, violence and despair as the citizens of one of the world's most beautiful cities were being in-

---

6. Franc-Tireurs et Partisans

exorably dragged into the chaos of war. People were turning to the blackmarket economy as wartime inflation plunged many Parisians into the poverty level. In doing so, they were become more and more exposed and, in turn, inured to the vices and excesses of the subculture. Sex, drugs and violence had become a way of life for many, and the Vichy regime was losing control of the madness.

The corruption was such that the influence of the Paris Mob and the fearsome Corsican Mob had spread throughout the Vichy network in Paris. As a result, Mob bosses had detailed knowledge of both police and military operations throughout the country. It was invaluable information in coordinating their smuggling and hijacking activities across France.

One particular item of note came as a bolt of inspiration to the Paris Mob bosses. They learned that the *maquis*, the informal network of peasants and farmers who had a community and code of honor similar to the Corsicans in the Old Country, were conspiring with the Resistance in a series of operations against the Nazis throughout Southern France.

One of their projects was a planned insurrection in the town of Tulle, which was already a beehive of insurgency. The word was that the Nazis had a major transport of morphine en route to Normandy, and it was being redirected to the General Hospital in nearby Brive rather than to risk its safety at the hospital in Tulle.

The rumor was that the morphine, valued at two million Reichsfrancs, was being delivered in a metal case under armed guard. The Mob knew that they could water down the product and put it on the streets of Paris for a return of four million francs. After calling an emergency meeting in a Parisian suburb and making numerous calls to the island of Corsica, the Mob families eventually decided on a game plan.

The Corsicans and the Parisians elected to turn the job over to their most notorious faction, the Bony-Lafont Gang, who in turn designated their top enforcer, Henri Lafont, to oversee the project. Lafont had just the crew in mind to get it done.

The five men scrambled from the military truck in front of the bustling hospital in the neighboring village of Brive amidst the chaos and the faraway thumps and crashes of mortar and rocket fire. Civilian, police and hospital personnel scrambled wildly as they prepared to evacuate the endangered town. The men, dressed in long white coats, rushed through the front doors of the lobby and shoved their way through the multitude to the reception desk.

"We've been sent to pick up and deliver the special transport," the leader, a tall, homely gray-haired man, announced to the head nurse.

"The special medicine?"

"The field supplies, you fool! Can't you see we're in a hurry?"

She directed them to a doorway leading to a corridor winding down to the basement level. The men raced down the hall to the rear loading dock where two medics were loading a small truck under guard by two Vichy soldiers.

"I am Dr. Renaud," the tall man announced. "I am here to take charge of the shipment."

"We've received no orders to release the shipment to anyone," one of the guards retorted. "We have been instructed to accompany these men to the next town."

One of the men, a swarthy, athletic man with thick black hair and dark eyes, stepped forth and fired his Beretta into the chests of the soldiers before shooting the medics in their heads.

"Now how are we supposed to use those uniforms?" a man with dark blond hair and a thick mustache stepped towards the bodies.

"It'll make you look like you've done something for your country, you oaf!" the gray-haired man snapped. "You two, get their coats. You other two, check to make sure the merchandise is there. Jacques, you drive."

"So I get to have you telling me how to get out of town," Jacques Tremblay snarled. "Why do I get the feeling you invited yourself along just to get a cut out of our share on top of your commission?"

"Maybe Paris didn't feel comfortable trusting you and your friends with such a valuable shipment," Germaine Lafont replied.

Lafont was one of the most powerful captains in the Parisian Mob, with strong connections with the dreaded Corsican Mob. Tremblay was the leader of one of Lafont's most dangerous crews, but theirs was a relationship balanced precariously by Tremblay's ruthless ambition and Lafont's depthless greed.

Jacques held his tongue as his gang loaded the truck and clambered inside. He was afflicted with an intermittent explosive disorder, symptoms of which included a sudden rush of blood to his head causing the veins in his temples to visibly pulsate. Lucien Belmondo, his right-hand man, patted him reassuringly on the shoulder as Jacques gunned the engine and sent the truck squealing down the road.

"Be careful!" Germaine barked. "Those vials are made of glass! Do you realize how much we stand to lose if one vial breaks?"

"They're packed in foam, Germaine," Jean-Paul Marat spoke up, lighting a cigarette.

"Did I ask you, you sot?" Germaine yelled at him. "And I told you not to light those cheap weeds of yours while we're riding together!"

"Hey, relax," Lucien interceded. "It's tense enough around here. We just wasted four people."

"Bloodless coward," Germaine snorted. "I've killed four people before breakfast."

"Back off, you Boris Karloff motherfucker!" Jacques screamed at him, filling the others with trepidation. Germaine's strong resemblance to the actor was such that it was only dared mention beyond his earshot.

"What did you say?" Germaine asked in disbelief.

"Who the fuck do you think you're talking to!" Jacques began to see red flashes before his eyes. "We're the toughest gang in Paris! The only reason you're riding with us is because of your brother! And I care about as much about him as I care about you!"

"Why, you worthless piece of shit," Germaine choked with rage. Jacques slammed the brakes, pulled his Beretta from his shoulder holster, and shot Germaine in the face in one violent motion. The others watched in shock as Jacques threw his door open and stalked around the truck, coming to a halt at a slope overlooking a creek in a gully below.

"This is it," Marcel Chouinard, a rotund man, squealed in despair. "Henri will have us all killed!"

"Shut up, Marcel," Jean-Paul clambered out of the truck along with Lucien. "We need to think this out."

"Okay," Lucien stood alongside Jacques, facing the gully. "We have to make it look like he got hit by the *maquis*. With all the fighting in the area, Paris may blow it off as an accident."

"Not Henri," Marcel whined as he clambered from the truck. "You killed his cousin. He'll kill us on principle."

"It could work," Jean-Paul mused. "With all the tension between the Mob and the Communists on the streets of Paris, we could make it look like the FTP put the *maquis* up to it."

"We got the morphine," Jacques stood with his hands on his hips. "Two million francs' worth."

"What'll we do with it?" Jean-Paul muttered. "With all the wounded troops coming back from Normandy, the Nazis will scour the countryside for it. If we escape, we'll have no choice but to bring it to Paris. Henri will have every gunman in the Mob looking for us, not to mention the Corsicans. We wouldn't last twenty-four hours."

"The politicals will pay for it," Jacques decided. "We'll sell to the highest bidder, FTP or FFI[7], I don't give a shit which one. Okay, Marcel, wipe up the mess, get all the blood and glass out of the truck. Jean-Paul, you drag that piece of shit down to the creek and give him to the fish."

"Maybe we should all get in and drive the truck into the creek," Lucien laughed.

"Could be a good idea," Jacques replied softly. "We'll see what happens."

He continued to stare down at the creek for a long, long time.

The British Empire had managed to keep a stiff upper lip despite the excesses of the Nazi Empire in trying to force them out of the war. The Nazis had bombed the British Isles more than any other target in the history of warfare, to no avail. Their V-2 rockets hailed down on a nightly basis, and the English lived in a state of terror, awaiting the air-raid sirens in the dark and the terrible loss unveiled by the dawn. Yet they refused to be cowed, abiding by their daily routine, not letting the war deny them the simple pleasures of life.

This spirit was in greatest evidence at night, when the London fog combined with the Nazi rockets' red glare to fill the city streets with foreboding. Nightclub owners lived in fear of a direct hit, though knowing that they continued to profit at risk while so many others were living hand-to-mouth. Patrons ventured out for evenings of dining and entertainment, wishing to escape the brutal realities of rationing, bomb shelters and razed neighborhoods. Families watched the revelers from their windows with mixed emotions, cursing their foolhardiness while cheering their indomitable spirits.

To those at the Hotel Europa, at times it was as if they lived in another dimension. Despite the intermittent blackout and terrific bomb blasts, life went on as usual against a resplendent background of plush carpeting, exquisite furniture

---

7. French Forces of the Interior

and fixtures, fine art and soothing music. Well-dressed clientele exchanged banter with the hotel personnel and rubbed elbows in the lobby before ordering dinner or retiring to the cocktail lounge for drinks and music.

A table of four, seated alongside the bandstand, had ordered a sumptuous dinner of steak, lobster, caviar and champagne as they took their turns on the dance floor. At length, they were approached by a waiter delivering a handwritten note. The two men at the table exchanged comments before summoning the waiter and paying the tab. They next led their dates outside the lounge where they were met by a powerfully built, dark-haired man. He joined them as they walked towards the elevators and took one to the third floor.

The two couples were led into an elegant suite at the end of a long hall by the thick-muscled Irish hood, closing the door behind them before preceding them towards the next room where he exchanged whispers with a tall, thin confederate. The husky man beckoned them into the next room where a third man awaited.

"So yer lookin' for some marijuana and ye got some money," the dark-eyed, swarthy man narrowed his eyes. "How much are ye lookin' fer?"

"How about a pound?" the blond, blue-eyed Englishman replied. "That'll be about a hundred pounds, and we don't do cheques," the Irishman smirked. There was nothing here that made him believe these were the kind of people who would be scoring serious weight.

"Okay," the blond reached into his pocket and produced a wallet and badge. "I'm Harry Blackburn with the British Secret Service. This building is under surveillance, and you're under arrest. The three of you, turn and put your hands against the wall now!"

A loud click caused Blackburn to break into a cold sweat. He turned to face a fourth man at the door behind them holding a sawed-off shotgun.

"Stupid Limey bastard," the husky man sneered, walking over and hauling off, dropping Blackburn across a glass coffee table with a right cross. The table shattered as Harry crashed to the floor, the swarthy man plucking his wallet from his hand.

"What've we got?" the curly-haired shotgun man trained his weapon on Harry's friends.

"This isn't Secret Service, it's some kind of military intelligence," the swarthy man muttered. "I thought Logan had this sort of thing taken care of."

"Jimmy, I've got two murder indictments staring me in the face," the thin man blurted. "I can't take this sort of heat!"

"Who's this little Yank piece of shite!" the husky man came over and tore the wallet out of Harry's partner's pocket. "Henry Geronimo? Is this a bloody Indian? And who are these whores?"

"I beg your pardon," the blonde woman managed.

"We're Military Intelligence," Henry cleared his throat. "This is Agent Monroe and Agent Mansfield."

"These whores have no ID," Jimmy tore through their purses.

"Let's throw 'em out the window along with these bastards."

"Are you nuts!" the thin man exclaimed.

"How the hell Logan put you on my team I'll not know," Jimmy snarled.

"Leave the drugs, walk out, we'll say you escaped," Harry gurgled, blood drooling from his mouth. "If they catch you with drugs we can't save you."

"If they catch us we're fecked, period," Jimmy reached behind a couch and produced a small satchel. "You three, have a seat on the couch by your friend. All three of you will count to a hundred, together, nice and loud. If we hear a one of you stop we'll come back and blow yer brains out."

"They'll see the satchel," Harry reasoned. "Leave it, I say."

"Feckin' Limey bastard!" Jimmy dropped the satchel on his face and kicked him as hard as he could in the groin as the women cried out.

The three of them too a seat as the Irishmen bolted out the door. Harry joined the chorus as best he could, the four of them following instructions. They next waited a short time before regaining their feet, Henry pulling Harry off the carpet.

"I say, that turned out to be one bit of adventure, eh?" Harry managed a smile. The blonde responded by hauling off and smashing him in the face, dropping him backwards onto the couch.

"You lousy shitbag!" she screamed. "You asked if we wanted to score some weed, not to risk our lives doing so! You better forget my number, and I ever see you again I'll bash your brains in! And that goes double from you, you Paki runt!"

"Actually I'm Apache, ma'am," Henry corrected her as she stormed out the door. Her friend stopped long enough to slap him hard across the face before leaving.

"Well, the more for us, I say," Harry staggered to his feet, opening the satchel to admire its contents.

"Welsh women," Henry rubbed his face. "What tempers."

"Is everything all right here?" a hotel manager came through the door with two security guards.

"Just a slight misunderstanding," Harry assured him. "One of our Irish friends arranged for us to meet a couple of girls here. We didn't seem to get on so well."

"I'll say," the manager grumbled as he stormed off. "Inform your friends the damage'll be added to the tab."

"They were big girls," Henry shrugged as the guards stared skeptically around the room.

"We're about three days' AWOL, y'know," Harry wiped his lip as Henry started out the door once the guards had left. "We'll have to do our best with this, can't bring it back, eh?"

"I wouldn't worry about it," Henry grinned. "There's still plenty of fun and adventure ahead in this war."

Neither of them could have any idea how prophetic his words would prove.

Chapter Three

Carl remembered back to what seemed to be a million years ago, back on a rainy day during Angie and his senior year at the University, before the war broke out, before he joined the SS. They had gone out to the lake that day, hoping it would not rain, but rented out a bungalow just in case. The rain came down as a shower, and they were forced to run from their canoe by the lake back to the cabin up the hill. They were thoroughly drenched but fell laughing into each others' arms. Carl went about building a fire as Angie made some tea with the box of groceries they brought along.

There was some scraps of newspaper they had used to pack their glass containers, and Angie unrolled a piece telling of British Prime Minister Chamberlain's confidence in Hitler's decision to cease hostilities in Europe.

"When will it end?" she murmured. They had long ago avoided discussing politics due to their personal feelings of patriotism, but the political scene had become increasingly controversial and difficult to avoid. "All the violence and hatred."

"There will always be violence and hatred," Carl finally got a couple of pieces of charcoal to ignite. "The most important thing is to be able to show others that kindness still exists. It gives others an example to follow."

"What happens if you are forced to be violent and hateful? Suppose there was a war and you were forced to be a soldier?" she stared out the window.

"I'm not sure that defending your country makes you that way," Carl walked over to where she stood. "If a man breaks into your home, you're not passing judgment by having to stop him."

"Carl, I'm so afraid that Hitler will start a war and you will be enlisted," she turned to him, her eyes misty.

"If there was one, I would enlist in service to my country," he looked out the window, "but after it was over I would only hope things would be what they are…between you and I."

"How could you say such a thing?" she asked softly.

"I've seen men come back from the last war with parts missing," Carl paced slowly across the room. "I would never want to think that you were resigning yourself to living life with a cripple, regardless of conscience."

"Carl Hansen, look at me!" she demanded, as he turned to face her. "I love who you are, far more than I love you for what you look like. There could never be a burden I would not bear at your side, never forget that."

"It would be the damage inside that I would not subject you to," he said quietly. "I've seen men grow ugly from what they endured. I would never ask you to endure that, because I would no longer be the man you grew to love."

"Don't question what I would endure," a tear rolled down her cheek as she turned away.

"I don't know what I did to deserve such love," he came up behind her and put his hands on her shoulders.

"You never had to do anything," she reached up and took his hand in hers.

"Angie, there could be no fight, no battle, no war that could ever stop me from coming back to you," he gently turned her around and took her in his arms. "And nothing will keep me from being the man you fell in love with. I would die before cheating you of that."

He recalled that everlasting kiss that followed, closed his eyes and tried to remember all, the scent of her hair, its luster against his face, her silky skin, her perfume, the feel of her body in his arms, pressed against his chest. He pulled out his wallet and gazed at her picture as he did so many times a day. He chuckled as he thought of first his schoolmates, then his Army buddies, chiding him that it was the picture of an actress he had, not his girlfriend at all.

He stretched out on his bed in his tent on the battalion campground outside Brive, resting before the next leg of the trek to Normandy. He knew there would be great bloodshed ahead, but he resolved to keep that promise to Angie. Somehow he would bring the young man from Gottingen back home, and leave the fighting man far behind him.

"Gentlemen, it seems we've got a bigger problem now."

Gunter Schweinberg had two of his men bring in a large radio that stood about a meter from the ground. They dutifully set up a large antenna and wired it to the radio amidst the catcalls and insults of Captain Kahn's platoon leaders before disappearing out the door.

The Regiment had moved into Brive on the evening of June 5th and wasted no time in quelling the local disturbances caused by the sudden appearance of the Waffen SS. Insurgents were rounded up and thrown in jail, homes searched and dozens of people interrogated. By the break of dawn the citizens of Brive had been thoroughly traumatized and in no shape to offer any resistance.

General Lammerding had given orders that the Division was to reassemble in the Limousin region by June 8th in preparation for their scheduled arrival at Normandy, and Colonel Stadler made certain that his staff understood their grave responsibility in meeting the deadline.

"Good morning, gentlemen," Major Wulf sauntered into the room as the Einsatzgruppen cadre left. "Gunter informed me that he had a rather interesting presentation this morning. He asked me to join you, and I accepted his invitation."

"Glad to have you, Major," Kahn brought him a cup of coffee. Carl noticed how Eric's reptilian monitoring of Gunter turned into a glazed look of indifference once Wulf stepped into the room. He was somewhat glad that Eric still respected the chain of authority. Eric was growing increasingly impudent around Kahn, and it was creating a heightened level of friction among the commissioned officers.

"This is what the peasants in the fields of this region are listening to," Gunter switched on the radio and fiddled with the dials. The room grew silent as an exotic, sultry wave of melody seemed to flood the room. The distinct voice of a black woman crooned a spiritual, almost sensuous tune while a piano hammered out a bass background and a guitar provided a cacophony of notes that seemed to enhance the dark, vibrant piece. The silence was broken at length as Eric began slapping the beat on his thigh.

"You're familiar with this?" Gunter could not help himself, and immediately regretted it as Eric's eyes narrowed.

"I'd daresay we've all heard it from time to time," Carl was quick to intercede.

"It makes all the sense in the world in your case, Carl," Wulf turned towards him. "A man who moves like a panther, fights like a lion and is as deadly as a snake must have some jungle instinct about him."

Carl grinned softly as the room broke into relieved laughter.

"This is Radio Bastille, coming to you from the liberated heart of France," a husky female French-speaking voice filled the room as the blues song faded away. "This is your fellow patriot, Madame Dominique, bringing you the best of Western culture and entertainment along with up-to-date news as our Allies come ever closer to bringing liberty and justice back to our homeland."

"What's she saying?" Peter Garthaffner asked, igniting a volley of sexual innuendos, catcalls and jeers before Gunter switched off the radio.

"She says she's tired of listening to boring Nazi Party bullshit," Eric smirked.

"Radio, gentlemen," Gunter said quietly. "The trend of the future. Our Fuhrer used it to usher in our Thousand Year Reich. Our armies brought it to a new level in coordinating our efforts in securing our interests across the planet. Only now our enemies have twisted it to spread decadence and insurrection, corruption and alienation across Europe. This may well be the most powerful weapon in their arsenal in their efforts to undermine National Socialism. We must make no mistake in underestimating the power of this new media. We must search out and destroy this network, and in doing so, break the spinal column of insurgency throughout southern France."

"So what's the solution?" Wulf inquired.

"Finding the location of these transmissions and closing down this radio network must become one of our major priorities," Gunter was emphatic. "This woman, Madame Dominique, must be regarded as an underground icon by these people. A person of such stature cannot remain hidden for long. Someone knows where she is, she has sponsors, she has friends. Once she is in our custody, she can be made to talk. And, gentlemen, I can guarantee you, she will talk."

"Gotta watch them frog women, they can give you warts," Eric snickered. "Isn't that right, Carl?"

"You know something, Eric?" Carl rose to his feet and pulled the sawed-off shotgun from its holster on his thigh. Heinz and Kahn were quick to box him in and calm him down.

"Eric, a word, if you will," Wulf rose, his face flushed with anger. "Gentlemen."

The commandos gave him lazy salutes as he led Eric out the door like a principal taking an unruly student to the office.

"Well," Gunter exhaled. "Where were we?"

"You're asking us to make it a priority to find out where some girl is playing records and bad-mouthing the government," Carl retorted. "I don't know if you realize that there are DJ's across America and England doing the same thing on a daily basis and getting paid for it. You can't take away people's freedom of speech and think there will be no backlash. It's man's most basic and cherished liberty. If you tell him he can't speak, read or think as he wants, he'll go somewhere and find someplace where he can. And if you confine him and deny him that right he will fight you tooth and nail as best he can. I've had this argument in the University over and over again until I was debating it in my sleep."

"The University of Gottingen?" Gunter said admiringly. "And what was your major?"

"Double major in education and literature, minor in art. I would've been teaching if it wasn't for this damned business," Carl sat back disgruntledly.

"Can you imagine!" Hans Beckmann cackled. " 'What is your problem, son?' BOOM!" he aimed and fired an imaginary shotgun.

"So what are you in real life, a comedian?" Carl smirked.

"Actually, my father is a jeweler. He had wanted to bring me into the trade for years, but I would have died before taking up anything so boring. Now, however, after all this…I would gladly sit in a quiet room and admire the beauty of anything in perfect tranquility for the rest of my life," Hans smiled ruefully, as the rest nodded in silent agreement.

"So you don't think this deserves any priority?" Gunter asked.

"We're letting ourselves get distracted by all the toys and games out here," Carl insisted. "The fight is with the Yanks and the Brits, not with these people. This is work for the police and the Gestapo, not the military. Let's go to the coast, wipe the bastards off the beach, go back to Berlin, collect our medals and go home."

His tirade was met by a thunderous roar and enthusiastic applause as his comrades all reached over to pat his shoulders.

"Duly noted," Gunter took notes, managing a smile. "Duly noted."

Jacques Tremblay and his men sat in a two-story barn about two kilometers outside of Brive that had been converted into a dance hall by the locals. It was controlled by the *maquis*, many of whom were of Corsican ancestry. Jacques felt strangely at home among the farmers of the area, and was more readily accepted as a result.

It was a sunny afternoon and the barn doors had been thrown open wide to let the summer breeze fill the room with the scent of the lilies of the field. The gang sat around a solid wooden table in the far corner of the room facing the door, Jacques in the corner seat so he could see everyone who came and went as well as the activity on the road leading to the barn. The farm itself was positioned on a hill overlooking a vineyard down in a valley affording it a breathtaking view of the entire region. The hill country and the trees and forests beyond were as silhouettes against a majestic sunny sky with billowing clouds providing intermittent shade from the warming sunbeams.

The barn itself grew busier as the afternoon crowd began to arrive. A trio consisting of an accordionist, a fiddler and a guitarist accompanied a harmonica player singing French folk songs and the new creole music from Louisiana in the USA. The owner, a native of Marseilles, was a Corsican with strong ties to the Unione Corse[1]. His kitchen was renowned throughout the area for its Marseilles-style cuisine and its supply of *pastis*, known as the 'Guinness of Southern France'. He came over and laughed and joked with the gang before sending them a complimentary bottle of champagne.

The band took a break as the waitress brought the chef's special to the table, swordfish in olive oil with ratatouille and saffron rice along with a freshly-baked loaf of Fougasse bread and Dagineau wine. They drank a toast with champagne before enjoying the savory white wine with their meal.

"You know, once we score on this deal, I'm not sure I wouldn't be against the idea of coming here to plant stakes and take what comes. This is heaven," Lucien Belmondo spoke around a mouthful of swordfish.

"You see that treeline over there?" Jacques pointed with his fork. "They would chop you up over here and throw your head over there, in those hills."

"Real appetizing, Jacques," Jean-Paul Marat nodded, looking up from his plate.

At once the radio was switched on as the band gathered by the outdoor garden for a wine break. Eventually the strains of *La Marseillaise*[2] could be heard as the restaurant owner had arranged the break to coincide with the start of the broadcast.

"Good afternoon, fellow patriots," a soft female voice gushed over the room. "This is Madame Dominique coming to you live from Southern France courtesy of Radio Bastille. We've got an exciting hour of patriotic anthems, blues music, inspiring literature and up-to-the-minute reports on our Allies' heroic efforts in breaking through the Nazi defenses at Normandy and teaming up with the

---

1. Corsican Mob
2. French national anthem

French Army in kicking the Boche out of France! It won't be long, my beloved countrymen, so let's join in prayer and keep the faith as the countdown continues towards our day of liberation!"

At once it seemed as if Jacques had been overwhelmed by a surge of inspiration. The reality of France's predicament as a vassal state to the Nazi Empire fully dawned on him, and made the concept of liberation ever more real to him. He was suddenly galvanized by a sense of patriotism, and it was almost as if the voice of Dominique sparked a sudden passion to join the fray and fight for something with true meaning, for perhaps the first time in his life.

"I got to use the phone," Jacques suddenly rushed from the table.

"Where's he going?" Marcel spoke through a mouthful of ratatouille.

"Probably checking on a horse. I don't see how he's going to pick up his money," Lucien shook his head.

"Monsieur," Jacques approached the owner at his table in the opposite corner by the long antique bar. "I would like to make a long distance call."

"Certainly," the owner obliged. "To who?"

"The Resistance."

"You know," the owner shoved his hands in his pockets and stared at the floor, "if you were caught by the Nazis they would kill you if you did not talk. If you did, I could lose everything, and there are people in this area who would not stop looking for you were that to happen."

"Okay, let's try this for size," Jacques met his gaze as he looked up. "You've heard about Germaine Lafont and the hijacking at Brive. Well, if that got out, that you met me, I would not stop looking for you."

"Here," the owner produced a pad and pencil, "is a number to call. The bartendress will bring a phone and connect you."

"This is Jacques Tremblay," his voice crackled over a poor connection. "I was given this number by a member of the *maquis* outside of Brive, Pierre Le Blanc. "I need to get a message to

Madame Dominique. Tell her I have the package and I want to make a deal."

"Hold on," a muffled voice faded from the phone.

"This is Agent Stern, British Intelligence. Are you Jacques Tremblay?" the man struggled with his French.

"Yes I am."

"Prove it or I hang up now."

"I am traveling with three men known as the Tremblay Gang from Paris. There were five of us, but the other man, Germaine Lafont, is no longer with us. His cousin Henri has a bounty on our heads. The only thing keeping us alive is the fact that the cargo in my possession has a street value of four million francs. I can either make a deal with the FFI or the FTP, it matters less to me."

"Dominique works for the FFI," Stern was brusque. "Why her?"

"I want to meet her. I'm a big fan. If she does not meet my price, I'll sell to the FTP."

"Okay," there was a pause. "How can we contact you?"

"I'll contact you tomorrow night," Jacques replied, then paused himself. "So you're backing the FFI."

"We're backing whoever can help us stop the Nazis. That includes you."

Jacques hung up.

"So we've got a deal," the thin, tubercular Jean-Paul Marat lit another cigarette. The gang had finished their meal and Jacques told them what he had done before indicating it was time to leave.

"We got shit," Jacques peered about the countryside for signs of detection. "I know how those limeys operate. They sell their ass to the highest bidder. It's all money, just like the Yanks. You heard that rumor about them putting a million francs behind whoever can take Das Reich out? Put two and two together. They buy this off us for two million, sell it to the Corsicans for three mil, they triple their investment."

"That's crazy, Jacques," Jean-Paul walked with him back to their vehicle. "That's exactly what the Allies don't want, this stuff hitting the streets. You said so yourself. They don't want to hand the country over to a generation of junkies."

"Maybe so, maybe not," Jacques opened the driver-side door. "Just don't put anything past the limeys or the Yanks, they don't give a damn about this country. Not that I do either."

"I think you'd rather make your deal with Dominique," Jean-Paul slipped into the car.

"Yeah," Jacques grinned. "So do I."

Sgt. Harry Blackburn and Sgt. Henry Geronimo arrived at their hotel in downtown London in the wee hours of the morning. They had enjoyed a memorable bar-hopping tour, sampling the best Irish whiskey and English ale available. They had planned to return to their rooms by midnight for a good night's rest before their classified meeting that morning, but lost track of time and decided that they would be pressed to arrive on schedule.

They were awakened at five o'clock in the morning by a series of resounding crashes as four beefy MP's stormed into their room. Upon identifying the special operations agents, they shoved them in turn into a cold shower before throwing their clothes at them and shoving them out the door. They howled in protest as they hopped into the elevator, pulling on their socks and underwear before donning their shirts. They were prodded through the lobby and out to the street, pedestrians gazing in astonishment as the men tried to pull on their pants before they were thrown into a waiting truck.

They were driven to the Northumberland Hotel where they were hurled from the truck and ushered through the door into the stately waiting area in the lobby. They managed to compose themselves before they were summoned into a conference room towards the rear of the main floor.

"Gentlemen," an adjutant introduced them as they stood at attention before a long table at which sat three officers. "This is Major Jepson of F Section[3], Major Philips of the American OSS (*Office of Secret Services), and Major Cointreau of the French Army. At ease, men."

"We have read with interest your respective dossiers as respects your involvement in numerous clandestine operations in the European Theatre of Operations," Jepson tapped the folders on the desk before him. "You seem to work well together and you have combined to complete your assignments in timely fashion. Nothing but positive feedback has come back to us. Our allies in North Africa have given us nothing but glowing reports. Our concern is the nature of your off-duty activities, which have much to be desired. As you know, gentlemen, this is an extremely unforgiving area of service which we deal in, and one mistake, careless or otherwise, might not only be your last but could cost the lives of many others."

"I assure you, Major, our duty to our countries is first and foremost..." Blackburn began.

"Shut the fuck up," Philips ordered.

"As you know," Jepson continued, "the Nazis are on the run in North Africa. The so-called Desert Fox, General Rommel, has been recalled to the ETO, and their network is collapsing as we speak. Our success continues along the coast

---

3. French Section

of Normandy across the Channel. We are fully confident that the invasion will be the first of many victories of the Allied forces as we continue on to Berlin in ending this war. However, our concern is that our clandestine activities in Southern France are not bearing as much fruit as we expected."

"Well, sir, with all due respect," Geronimo offered.

"If we want your opinion we'll give you one!" Philips thundered.

"We're having a lot of problems over there that have to be resolved," Jepson was emphatic. "Things are going awry because we don't have anyone over there with the authority to coordinate our efforts. The conservative right-wing factions in France suffered a compound fracture, if you will, when Jean Moulin was murdered by Klaus Barbie and the Gestapo in Lyon last year. More and more right-wing extremists are siding with the Nazis in a backlash against the growing Communist underground movement. We've got Violette Szabo over there working with the FFI, she's doing a fantastic job but she's taking too many risks. She's taking too much of a personal interest, trying to avenge her husband's death. There are too many factions in the Limousin region, too many cooks in the kitchen. Our American cousins have made a sizeable investment in matching our funding, but we're trying our best not to hand it over to the Commies. Unfortunately, right now they're the only ones out there getting anything done."

"Right now SOE's sitting on over four million dollars, two million of which is Uncle Sam's money," Major Philips pointed out, staring at Geronimo. "I don't have to tell you what's going to happen if that money ends up going sideways in a wartime economy. There'll be an investigation leading to a court martial, and I can guarantee you that I will personally prosecute the guilty party to the fullest extent of the law, to say the least."

"We're planning on inserting you in the Paris theatre of operations, where you'll be briefed before moving on to Limousin," Jepson continued. "We're going to arrange a meeting with the FTP chief, Gilles Guevremont. We want you to carry the Commies for a few more rounds until we can get the FFI into the game. We're expecting full support from the *maquis*, they don't want to see the Commies in power either but they'll back whoever gets the job done. You'll keep the FTP on life support, just enough to keep their heads above water."

"Guevremont's a smooth bastard," Major Cointreau warned.

"He likes women, wine and song, most of all fine clothing. Be sure you keep a running total on him or he'll be tossing our money down on the Champs de Elysees."

"Uh, there will be funds for business expense?" Blackburn ventured. "We'll have to deal from a position of authority or they'll think we're bluffing."

"Don't think we're handing you a blank check," Jepson advised. "You're representing your governments and we expect you to play the role. Guns and ammo aren't coming cheap these days, however, and there'd better be more than enough to go around after all's said and done."

"You're a couple of fuckups, we know that," Philips glared. "We want Guevremont to think he'll pull the wool over your eyes. Only you need to make him think you're expecting it, and you won't make it easy. Hopefully all the jacking around will give the frogs...uh...sorry, Major...our FFI friends time to come to Jesus."

"No harm," Cointreau smiled. "As long as you Yank bastards deliver."

"You heard the man," Philips growled at them. "Get to it."

The commandos saluted smartly and marched out of the room, laughing and hugging once they left the building.

"We'll have the time of their lives!" they howled with glee.

It would be an experience they would remember for the rest of their days.

The men in black made their way through the dark hallways of the villa after having driven through numerous checkpoints and negotiated the ubiquitous security teams along the way. They were finally confirmed by two hulking guards at the doorway of the master bedroom on the upper floor before they were permitted entry.

"Finally made it," the darkened figure growled from the shadowy table by the window. "I thought I'd be up all night. What took you so long?"

"Quite a bit of security around here, I'd say," the taller of the trenchcoated men spoke. "Were you expecting assassins?"

"I haven't made a whole lot of friends around here since my injury," Robert Ruess replied. "Not that I was very popular in the first place."

"You've brought a lot of attention to your situation," the slender man replied. "That must pass."

"What must I do?" Ruess rose from his chair.

He stepped forth from the table into the dim light, and both men were visibly stunned. The third-degree burns on his face had seared most of the flesh to the bone, and various ointments and treatments had done little to prevent the continuous flow of fluids from the open wounds. Most of the skin had been reduced to a mass of purplish tissue, and his features had been disfigured beyond recognition. He was forced to stare in order to focus on objects, and his lips had retracted so as to expose his teeth in a perpetual snarl. His scalp had been burned past his ears so that his hair sat in a tangled mess at the back of his head.

"You know why we're here, and we know why you summoned us," the men followed Ruess out the hall to the drawing room at the end of the corridor. He was still recovering from his injuries from his crucifixion in Russia. His wrists were heavily bandaged and he required a cane to walk on his bandaged feet.

"I have given my life to my country and my Fuehrer," Ruess turned to face them as he strode to the head of an oaken study table in the middle of the room. "For that, I have gotten this in return. I deserve more than this, I want to enter the sacred brotherhood. I've earned the right."

"Don't you think you've given enough?" the tall man asked.

"I want the enemies of the Reich to suffer as I've suffered. I want to protect and defend our future generations from the evil that has caused me to suffer."

"Then we will show you the way."

The men produced a satchel from which they produced two candles, a copy of *Mein Kampf,* a gun and a dagger. The tall man stood at the table facing Ruess as the small man lit the candles.

"In the name of our Fuehrer, Adolf Hitler," the tall man spoke, "we gather here in fellowship to accept our SS brother, Robert Ruess, into the sacred and unbroken circle of the ODESSA[4]. Although we are all SS to the death, in the ODESSA we are reborn to fight the eternal struggle against Bolshevism and bring the truth of National Socialism to generations to come. Robert Ruess, do you accept this responsibility and duty to your Fuehrer, your race and your country?"

"I do."

The tall man took Ruess' right hand, placed it on *Mein Kampf,* then took his left hand and sliced the ball of his thumb with the dagger.

He placed a tissue in Ruess' hand, then took a candle and set the tissue on fire.

"Repeat," ordered the tall man. "This is how I will burn if I betray the sacred circle of ODESSA."

---

4. Organization of Former SS Members

Ruess did so.

"Robert Ruess, by the authority invested in me by the sacred brotherhood of ODESSA, I declare you to be a Werewolf of the clan and a knight of our invisible army. Remain ever faithful, ever vigilant, and obedient unto death."

"I will."

"You will not know where we are or when we will come to you," the tall man concluded. "You will know our voice when we call to you, and we will know when you are in need. As you prove yourself worthy, you will come to a greater knowledge and understanding of who and what you have become, and what and who we really are."

"So be it."

Ruess walked the men to the front door and bade them farewell, standing at the threshold until they drove off.

"What a crock of shit," Ruess laughed at his Einsatzgruppen guards, who obligingly laughed along with him. He retired to bed and slept the most restful sleep he had since the crucifixion, filled with dreams of revenge, power and glory beyond what he had ever dared imagine.

* * *

The limousine pulled up in front of the fashionable hotel along the outskirts of Brive amidst a cordon of security provided by a half dozen vehicles and a squad of armed men. They converged upon the limousine, pulled the passengers from the car and interrogated them thoroughly as the rear door was pulled open. A pallet bearing a covered figure was brought forth and carried into the hotel.

The pallet was rushed into the hotel and carried up a flight of stairs where another group of armed men awaited. They took possession of the pallet and brought in into a spacious suite directly to the large bedroom. A nurse was available to tend to the man on the pallet, who had been badly beaten and disfigured just hours ago.

"There are broken bones everywhere, including his neck and back," the nurse insisted. "I can give him a mild pain-killer without knocking him out but he must be brought to hospital."

"I only need fifteen minutes," a tall, elegant man replied. "Let it wait."

The man known as Gilles Guevremont was a tall, blond Frenchman who was the Communist Party secretary in Paris and the leader of the FTP forces in Southern France. He held a degree in political science from the University of Paris and was a qualified terrorist leader after having undergone extensive training in Russia. He had no vices other than his penchant for expensive designer clothing, which his position and his office in Paris allowed him to indulge.

"His condition may become critical if he isn't evacuated soon," the nurse warned.

"Comrade, can you hear me?" Guevremont sat at the man's bedside. His face was beaten beyond recognition and there were traces of blood seeping through the sheet despite the heavy bandaging.

"They beat me bad, Comrade," the man gasped. "I'm not going to make it."

"Of course you will," Guevremont patted his hand. "Now, how did they get onto you? It should have been a simple matter to intercept the drug smugglers after they left the hospital, there's only one road leading out of town."

"I have no idea," he whispered agonizingly. "It wasn't the army and it wasn't the police. They were dressed in black, but it didn't look like regular SS. They set up a decoy, we thought the hijackers had car trouble and we investigated. They lined us up and asked who was in charge. When no one answered they shot the first man. I admitted I was the leader and they killed the others. I was taken to a farmhouse, where they did this to me."

"Monsieur," the nurse warned. "He will go into shock unless I ease the pain."

"Get her out," Guevremont ordered one of his men. "Comrade, stay with me. Who did you see? What do you remember?"

"The leader," the man's eyes glazed over. "His face was horrible, covered with scars. They were all wearing black hats but the leader was giving orders and directing the torture. They asked me where the morphine was but I gave them nothing, not even about the hijackers. I only regret that I will not live to see the liberation of France!"

"It's probably his heart," one of the gunmen stepped over and felt the man's carotid artery. "He's gone."

"All right," Guevremont said evenly. "Get the nurse out of here, send her to Tulle, she will be useful in supplying information from there. Dispose of this fellow, send some money to his family. Have our contacts in Lyon find out who Skullface is. He is obviously the Nazis' counterinsurgency leader within the

Division. He's probably the one who had the FFI leaders ambushed the other night. I want this man assassinated. He's hiding in the dark, we have to draw him out."

"He could have lived," the nurse glared as she was ushered out the door.

"So can you," Guevremont shot back. "Do as you're told."

"Suppose he is on a secret mission?" his bodyguard asked. "They won't have anything."

"We'll find him. How could they hide a man so ugly?

"Just as we hide a man so beautiful."

There was a long silence before the gunmen shared a hearty laugh.

Chapter Four

"Where's the party?" Heinz Barth grunted.

It was the morning of June 9, 1944 by the time the Leader Regiment rumbled onto the outskirts of Tulle. Vichy sympathizers had informed their contacts in Lyon that the FTP was planning a major attack and were expected to derail the advance of the Kingdom Division for at least a day, buying more time for the Allied Expeditionary Force at Normandy. The Regiment had no idea that the attack had already taken place and that the garrison had been completely wiped out.

"Looks like there was one hell of a party," Carl growled as he stood on the opposite side of the turret of a Panzer tank, a good distance ahead of the main column rolling towards the village. "Think everyone's in bed with hangovers?"

"The 95th Security Regiment is stationed here," Heinz jacked a shell into the chamber of his rifle. "That's a lot of soldiers making sick call."

The commandos leaped from the tank and guarded one another's movement as they crept into town. They could see movement behind curtains in windows on upper floors of buildings leading to the town square, causing them to slink from door to door in moving up the street. They used hand signals to maneuver one another to every street corner, and made certain there was no sign of enemy before proceeding.

Upon reaching Champs de Mars they were astonished by the spectacle before them. A platoon of German soldiers lay in grotesque positions of death across the plaza, forty men having been beaten, shot, stabbed, strangled and mutilated by the terrorists. Some men had their genitals cut off and stuffed in their mouths. Others were covered in excrement. One soldier had holes in his heels through which a rope had been drawn; he had been dragged from a car bumper until his face was torn off. Signs and placards proclaiming French liberation and anti-German sentiment were festooned around the area, along with debris including broken furniture, wine bottles, and the bloodied garments of the slain soldiers.

"There's movement in the windows," Heinz circled in furtive patterns across the cobblestones, rifle at the ready. "I don't see any hostiles."

"Let's fall back and signal the advance units," Carl growled. "Let the ground units secure the area, they can reassemble the GMR and the Gestapo and let them handle this."

"Somebody's got to pay for this," Heinz snapped as he covered Carl's retreat.

"Let's just hope it's not the wrong people," Carl muttered.

It was later discovered that the insurgent attack began on 0500 on June 7th, and the besieged garrison managed to hold out until 1600 on the following day after 139 soldiers were killed and 40 wounded. The wounded had been dragged to the Champs de Mars where they were slaughtered in broad daylight.

The Panzer tanks rolled into town, taking strategic positions around the village as armored personnel carriers followed them in. They secured the area in awaiting the arrival of GMR troops, who proceeded door-to-door in search of terrorists, who had long since vanished. The Gestapo, however, had an updated list of known and suspected collaborators forwarded from Klaus Barbie's office in Lyon, and that led to the arrest of ninety-nine villagers on charges of assault and murder of military personnel. The villagers were taken to a nearby barracks where they were duly processed and tried by an SS court. Before long they had been convicted and sentenced to capital punishment.

* * *

Jacques Tremblay ran.

He and his gang pulled up along the outskirts of Tulle slowly after dark that evening and were mystified by the deathly silence. Gone were the patriotic banners, the French tricolor, the anti-Nazi signs and placards. Gone were the reveling crowds and blaring music. All that remained was shadows and the whistling wind. Jacques told them to park along the treeline so that he could sneak into the village to investigate. He crept along the bushes and eventually slipped into the shadows in making his way into an alleyway leading towards the thoroughfare.

He splashed softly through the mud and kicked something that had a weird feel to it. He looked down and was startled by the sight of the outstretched arm of a dead man in a dark suit. He stared hard into the shadows and realized that it was one of a stack of bodies piled against the brick wall like cordwood.

The vein in his temple began throbbing as he realized that the Nazis had hit Tulle and went on a killing spree. He crept towards the alley entrance and peered out slowly, ensuring that the street was deserted. As he stepped out into the darkness, he was astonished and enraged by the sight.

He saw the figures dangling from the lampposts and realized they were people who had been lynched by the SS. He rushed into the street and nearly stumbled on objects strewn across the cobblestones. He realized that the streets were covered by dead crows that had been killed by grieving relatives of the victims, hurling stones to prevent the scavengers from defacing the corpses.

He soon became overwhelmed by an uncontrollable fury that caused the blood in his head to pound his temples like triphammers. He clenched his fists against his temples and ran wildly down the street, his intermittent explosive disorder threatening to drive him berserk. He ran until he could run no more, and eventually realized that the rows of hanged men on lampposts stretched as far as the eye could see.

"You!" a voice called from the darkness. "Stop right there!"

A flashlight beamed on him as a GMR soldier came forth from the darkness, pointing a pistol at him.

"You can be killed for breaking curfew! What are you doing out here! Let me see your papers!"

"I'm looking for my…father," Jacques replied, reaching into his jacket. "Don't shoot."

The GMR trooper came closer, and Jacques whipped out his Beretta and shot the man five times in the head and chest. He stripped the man of his Luger pistol and an ammo clip before bolting and running in the direction of the sound of squealing tires along the opposite side of the street.

"What happened?" Lucien yelled from behind the wheel.

"They hung everybody," Jacques breathed heavily as he jumped into the passenger seat. "There are bodies hanging from every lamppost on the street. I just shot one of those GMR rats. They're back in control. We got to get out of here."

"Where to?" Lucien gunned the engine.

"Limoges," Jacques accepted a flask of whiskey from Jean-Paul. "I need to make contact with the Resistance. The Nazis are through playing games. We need to make this deal, sell this shit and get the hell out of France."

"Get out of France?" Lucien was dubious. "We need to talk."

"You stay here and talk to the Nazis, or Bony and Lafont, or whoever's left to talk to," Jacques took a large swig of whiskey. "I don't care where I go, but I've had my fill of this."

"What about the gang, Jacques?" Marcel was panicky. "We've been together since we were kids! We always said we'd always be together! We've made it through thick and thin, why all of a sudden are we talking like this!"

"Take it easy," Lucien assured him. "We said we'd talk."

There was a new radio station in town.

Radio Utopia brought a breath of fresh air into the region of Limousin. Its jazz-oriented format was punctuated by patriotic French songs that filled the hearts of both young and old with new hope. The new disc jockey, Madame Natasha, had a voice every bit as seductive as that of Madame Dominique, but her messages were far more aggressive and her news clips more informative. The people of Limoges crowded around their radios for the evening broadcast, exhilarated by its format. The guards posted at the doors of their meeting places watched cautiously for signs of the GMR, yet listened intently in order to share in the excitement that Radio Utopia was creating.

"This is a little something for Captain Skullface," the sultry voice cooed over the airwaves. "We know that you are the true face of Nazi Germany, not all those blond, blue-eyed bikers the Reich has been sending down the road for the showdown with the Allied forces. You should know by now that you can never crush the spirit of the French people. For every Frenchman and woman you round up in your trucks to meet with the Butcher, Klaus Barbie, two more will rise in defense of this proud and brave country. Just remember, when you come running back from the Atlantic with your tails between your legs, there will be twice as many people standing to block your path."

"Boyo!" Sgt. Harry Blackburn shook his fist exuberantly. "That'll have the kraut bastards stewing in their juice, wouldn't you say?"

He sat with Sgt. Henry Geronimo and Socialist Party leader Gilles Guevremont in the deserted restaurant at the Grand Hotel in the downtown area of the quaint village about thirty kilometers from the underground broadcast station.

They had the radio brought to them as they sipped cognac during their scheduled meeting that evening. They tapped their fingers on the armrests of their overstuffed provincial-style chairs as Madame Natasha played a particularly raucous Count Basie number on Radio Bastille.

"They should consider the fact that the Nazis are going to be on them like flies on shit after this," Geronimo sniffed. "Something like this is a slap in the face. Captain Skullface already has his death squads scouring the countryside looking for the insurgents after what you did in Tulle. When he hears this they'll be bringing people in for nothing but reprisals."

The OSS had double agents in Abwehr[1] who were instructed to search the medical records for casualties among officers assigned to the Das Reich Division and the Limousin region. They narrowed the search down to officers suffering facial injuries who had not been evacuated to Germany and soon decided upon Ruess. SOE agreed to a one hundred thousand mark bounty on Ruess, which was as much as that authorized on Lt. Carl Hansen for the assassination of twelve FFI leaders just days ago.

"The only ones hiding in the countryside are the *maquisards*," Guevremont insisted. "Our people are the true insurgents, standing guard by day and spreading chaos by night. You see, gentlemen, the French are not like the English, we do not share your prudent tendencies. Nor are we like the Americans, we do not explain ourselves before we act. We are more like the Latins, although our assassins are far more cerebral. We are distracting the Nazis, running them through the gauntlet before their battle with the expeditionary forces, the bull through the *corrida*, if you will. This is the red cape that maddens the bull, making him charge wildly towards disaster. And, of course, your generous contributions to our cause make it all the more disastrous."

"Let us try and remember that we have already contributed a quarter-million francs to your organization," Blackburn folded his hands in his lap and he sat back pensively. "This is quite a bit of money. Of course, we can hardly expect your men to charge out against the Das Reich Division like a swarm of lemmings, but then again, it shouldn't resemble a game of hide and seek. They've been cruising down the road to Normandy as if on an excursion in most places. I daresay, at times it doesn't seem as if there's an insurgency at all."

---

1. German military intelligence

"I don't think that is a fair assessment, Sergeant," Guevremont protested. "I think that Madame Natasha is making it very clear that the Nazis may be traveling a one-way road to destruction. Those convoys of armored trucks headed for the coast may not be as fearsome in retreat. They will also be carrying a fair share of wounded, and their soldiers will have had more than their share of the bitter vetch of defeat. You can be sure we will be waiting, and the vengeance of Lyon will blacken our hearts."

"The point is that we're not going to need help after the fact," Geronimo emphasized. "We've got Eisenhower, Montgomery and Patton waiting to hammer the Nazis all the way back to Berlin once we gain a foothold here. What we're doing here is trying to weaken the Nazis in order to save lives on the coast."

"All right," Guevremont conceded. "I can put a brigade on the road to Oradour. We'll need high explosives and bazookas, and money for payoffs and supplies once the Nazis recover."

"Oradour," Blackburn frowned. "That's a good ways from the coast. If you don't hit them hard enough you might have to hit them again, and they'd be better prepared."

"We'll hit them hard enough," Guevremont insisted. "They'll never know what did hit them."

"Do you think this is worth another quarter-million of the taxpayers' money?" Geronimo asked Blackburn. The SOE had financed the Tulle operation at a cost of two hundred fifty francs with impressive results.

"That raises the stakes to a half-million," Blackburn mused. "If we up the ante for another half-million upon completion of a successful mission, then our friend here would have to deliver or get off the...pot, eh?"

"A million francs," Guevremont grinned. "Gentlemen, we will blow them clear up to the coast for that kind of money."

"There's nothing about the Das Reich that makes us look forward to it," Geronimo stared at him. "Do remember that."

"Here's a poser," Blackburn arched his eyebrows. "Once the war is over, we'll have this rivalry between the conservatives and the socialists to contend with...and, of course, an extremely powerful and aggressive Soviet Union along the Eastern front. They may well be able to add a lot of weight to an argument as to which way France might veer politically. The point being, *Monsieur*, is that we really don't want to have to deal with the problem of having to come back in here to take our guns back."

"I can assure you, Sergeant," Guevremont insisted, "the Socialist Party in France is dedicated to the liberation of our country and the unity of our people in rebuilding our nation."

"We'll drink to that," Blackburn raised his glass.

"We'll drink to anything," Geronimo chortled.

"That's what I'm afraid of," Guevremont muttered.

"What's that?" they demanded.

"To France!" Guevremont raised his glass exuberantly.

Nearly twenty kilometers away, the strains of Count Basie's orchestra died away before Madame Natasha began playing a new piece by Louis Armstrong and his band on Radio Utopia. Jacques Tremblay turned down the volume a notch to the consternation of his crew as they sat around the living room of the rural cottage that served as a safe house for the *maquisard* network.

"I'm worried about the repercussions this will cause," Jacques shook his head regretfully. "The Nazis will come down hard on the insurgency for this. Madame Dominique will become a major target. They will be trying to tear the entire network apart."

"You've really fallen for this woman's voice," Jean-Paul Marat shook his head.

"What has that to do with anything?" Jacques growled. "If they kill her, all our plans will go to hell. Who will we take this deal to, the Communists? If we take it back to Paris the Corsicans will cut our heads off. Unless you'd like to sell it back to the Germans."

Jean-Paul Marat looked at him pensively. Jacques had sworn himself to hate politics. This sudden stance against the Communists was something totally unexpected.

"Why can't we trust in Monsieur Le Blanc?" Marcel Chouinard entreated him. "He is a good man, he's allowed us the use of this cottage. Surely he can speak to someone in the *Maquis* on our behalf."

"And then what?" Jacques snapped. "He'll broker our deal for two million francs' worth of morphine, is that right? What do you think the *maquisards* will do with it, start dealing to the farmers out here? They'll go straight to Paris, and then what? Perhaps Henri Lafont will send an army down here as an escort for the two million, along with his regrets that we were forced to kill his brother!"

"Lighten up, Jacques," Lucien Belmondo lit a cigarette. "We can't control what's happening, there's a war going on."

"We control *this*," Jacques nodded towards the aluminum suitcase against the far wall. "Everyone wants it: the Nazis, the socialists, the communists, the Allies, the Corsicans, the Paris Mob. We have to play this like a card game. No bluffs, no bad moves, never show our hand. If we play this right we walk away with a half million francs apiece. There will be no place in the world we couldn't go: Algeria, Morocco, Spain, Canada, even America."

"We travel together, we set up shop with all the money," Jean-Paul had been as concerned as Marcel about Jacques' remarks on splitting up the gang. "We split four ways, if we pool our resources in another time and place we're back at two million. It's a lot of money, we could even invest in a legitimate enterprise and go straight."

"What do you think, Jacques?" Marcel was elated by the idea.

"Sounds like fun to me," Jacques shrugged. "I'd like get an office in the Empire State Building myself."

"Now we're talking," Jean-Paul said encouragingly.

Robert Ruess stood at the drawing room window of his chateau that evening, lifting weights with increasing capacity. His wrists were on the mend and his trainer, a sports physician from Berlin, was treating him as a professional athlete needing an early return to the field. Regular injections of Novocaine and cortisone were making it easier for him to work with his damaged wrists and feet.

His visitor had arrived and was escorted to the upper quarters by an SS rifleman. The man in the black coat and hat was impressed by the tiger-muscled frame of the black-clad Ruess, though the disfigured face was still difficult to gaze upon.

"So, I hear you've got some new developments to talk about," Ruess carefully wiped his forehead, trying to avoid ripping any blistered skin open.

"I see your training is progressing quite well," the ODESSA agent nodded. "Hopefully you'll be able to refrain from taking to the field yourself, as you've been prone to do in the past. We have more than enough personnel ready and willing to prove themselves just as you have in countless situations."

"Yes, I do have my fair share of medals," Ruess grinned. "I'm what you might call a take-charge type of fellow. Why take a chance of somebody else mucking up a job when you get it done right yourself?"

"People like you are becoming increasingly irreplaceable," the agent replied. "As Friedrich Nietzsche once said, why act alone when you can multiply your efforts by getting a bunch of zeros to stand behind you?"

"Take that up with Carl Hansen," Ruess chuckled. "He sees things the same way I do, and we've both collected about the same amount of medals and registered kills with similar success ratios. He likes going out alone like I do for the same exact reason. Word around the campfire was that he took out about twelve FFI leaders at a secret meeting a couple of nights ago. He walked away with a ton of information that we would've never gotten if a bunch of amateurs went in and shot the place up."

"Be that as it may," the agent waved his hand dismissively. "The reason for my visit is the heightened blackmarket activity in this area. The Division's movement across the region has the insurgents coming out of the woodwork like cockroaches. They're moving quite a bit of contraband, and there are two particular shipments that have attracted our attention."

"Do tell," Ruess began curling a 35-pound dumbbell.

"One of the shipments has literally become part of urban legend in these parts. As you may or may not know, ODESSA is involved in a major financing operation in South America in the event that the war does not end in our favor. We have invested millions of francs in the German colonies across the continent, and essentially it's a win-win situation. If we come out victorious, the colonies will be centers of influence as the boundaries of the Reich spread across the globe. If we lose, heaven forbid, there will be bases around the world from which ODESSA can ensure the survival of National Socialism."

"So what, the terrorists grabbed one of your shipments?"

"Due to the secret nature of our organization, sometimes the left hand does not know what the right is doing. In this case, we were informed that two million francs' worth of gold bars may have been seized by the terrorists. We do not know the shipment's point of origin, who or where it was authorized, or even its destination. What we do know is that one of the leaders of our organization has reported it missing."

"Thank the Lord for our sophisticated intelligence network," Ruess scoffed.

"What makes it more interesting is that a transport of morphine scheduled to be shipped to the Normandy front was recently hijacked at a hospital in Brive. It had an estimated value of two million francs. The word is that it fell into the hands of Corsican gangsters, who are negotiating a deal for it with the terrorists. Now, logic dictates that the terrorists may not have two million francs to spare. Our sources indicate that the SOE may have up to three million francs budgeted for terrorist operations. They are not going to turn two-thirds of it over to a band to drug smugglers. Where else would they get the money? They must have the gold somewhere."

"Where do you think it is?" Ruess finished his set of curls.

"According to sources, the Oradour area is used as a major storage resource by the terror network. If the terrorists continue to launch attacks against our troops in the same manner as they did in Tulle, then it would justify a retaliatory action on our part. This could allow your men to conduct searches and seizures and recover not only our assets but anything else that could…further our own interests."

"Consider it done," Ruess grinned evilly.

"Again, we caution you to remain under cover in directing this operation," the agent admonished him. "The GMR informed the Gestapo that a mid-level Parisian gang leader was abducted and tortured in the Brive area shortly after the hijacking incident. The Gestapo has no record of this. He and a few others have been taken to a place the terrorists are referring to as the House of Pain. Our friends would wonder if I am not standing in this House of Pain."

"Well, it's definitely not the fun house, but I don't know about any torture chambers, unless the last fellow had one," Ruess shrugged.

"There is also an issue over a bounty having been placed on the head of a man they call Captain Skullface."

In a flash Ruess bounded across the room and grabbed the agent by the throat, producing a dagger which he used to compress the man's tongue. The stranglehold, the blade and the close-up sight of Ruess' leaking burns gave the agent a panic attack.

"Okay, listen up. If my own mother ever called me that, I would cut off her head and throw it in the street. Now you go back and tell our people, everyone stationed here in Frogland, and all the frogs, cops and robbers alike. Got it?"

He managed to nod his head, eyes bulging with fright. Ruess released him and he collapsed back in his chair.

"Go back to wherever you came from and tell your superiors that I'll have this taken care of in forty-eight hours, one way or the other."

The agent managed to give the Nazi salute before bolting out the door. Ruess nearly doubled over with laughter as he heard the man choking his way down the hall.

He ended his workout with four sets of two hundred twenty-five-pound bench-presses, then retired to his room for a shot of cognac and some Mozart before bedtime. He had some long, long days ahead, to which he eagerly looked forward.

Jacques Tremblay met with the agents beneath a lamppost on a darkened street along the edge of town that night. They ushered him into a waiting car, placed a burlap sack over his head and instructed him to rest his head on his arms on the rear of the passenger seat as they drove to their destination. Jacques cursed and swore as he was pulled from the car and led across a field to a cottage outside of town before the hood was removed.

He was led inside and surrounded by a group of armed men who searched him thoroughly, relieving him of his Beretta and a switchblade.

"She is expecting you," a beefy gunman warned him. "If she so much as raises her voice, or if we hear no sound, we're coming in. Expect the worst."

Jacques entered the dimly-lit room which appeared as a woman's boudoir. He crossed the thick burgundy shag carpet towards a curtained dais in the far corner where the silhouetted figure
of a woman sat.

"Monsieur Tremblay," the woman greeted him.

"I'd recognize that voice anywhere," Jacques smiled, standing about one-third meter away from the opaque veil. He figured her to be about one and two-third meters tall with a healthy physique.

"We have been informed you have the shipment everyone is looking for. We are highly impressed by the fact you've eluded the German Army, the police and Gestapo, as well as the Corsicans, all this time."

"Well, I told my gang that I wasn't going down without meeting you first."

"I'm flattered, Monsieur. Now to business. There are a lot of issues surrounding the merchandise in your possession."

"We've gone over all the angles. I want two million for the merchandise."

"Monsieur Tremblay," she said quietly, "we don't have two million."

"How much do you have?"

"We don't have anything. Everything we have is tied up in fighting the Nazis."

"Hold on," Jacques fumed. "I know the Yanks have three million floating around out here somewhere. Plus I know that the bourgeoisie in Paris are sending a ton of money down here to keep you people in business. You can't tell me you can't give me anything for this stuff. And, I know the FTP would drop a few francs on this...given the chance."

"Monsieur Tremblay..."

"Jacques."

"Jacques," she continued. "The Vichy government and the Gestapo have Paris in a state of virtual martial law. Anyone is subject to arrest, search and seizure at any time. They can torture and murder anyone suspected of subversion. Money comes to us in trickles at best. Plus, the Allies are still qualifying prospective groups for their investments. They've already given almost a million francs to the Communists. They're trying to resist giving them much more, but if we can't put anything on the table they may give up on us."

"Come on, Dominique," Jacques reasoned. There's got to be something in it for me."

"Okay," she relented. "If you turn the shipment over to us, we will guarantee you new identities and positions in a new Republican government once the war is over. You'll be able to start new lives and rest assured of a secure income for the rest of your lives."

"We're pretty set in our ways," Jacques exhaled. "I don't know if this'll fly too high with my guys."

"Please reconsider," she entreated him. "If you sell it to the Communists they will almost certainly take power after the war with the Allies' endorsement. If you sell it back to the Mob they'll resell it to our children on the streets of Paris."

"I got to go back to my friends with this," he decided. "I'll call you. One thing, though, if I do this thing for you...I want to see you."

"What...what do you mean?"

He moved the curtain aside as she tucked her chin tightly against her chest.

"If I scream they will come for you," she warned him. "Don't do this."

"I'm not going to hurt you," he assured her. He put his finger on her chin but it would not budge.

"It's okay," he stepped away and slowly headed for the door. "I don't have to see your face, I know you are beautiful."

"Thank you," she murmured.

"I'll call you," he said merrily as he returned to the custody of her guards.

The town of Limoges was in a state of exultation.

Nazi flags were being torn asunder and burned throughout town, replaced by the French *bleu, blanc et rouge*[2] tricolor. Patriotic songs blared through loudspeakers along with live and recorded broadcasts of both Radio Bastille and Radio Utopia. Police and security personnel were being dragged into the street, stripped and beaten by vengeful townsfolk chafing under the yoke of Vichy rule. Police and military armories were set ablaze, their weapons caches confiscated by the *maquis*.

"This is an incredible victory," Gilles Guevremont said exultantly as he walked along the town square. Sgt. Harry Blackburn and Sgt. Henry Geronimo accompanied him on his victory walk, a phalanx of armed guards close behind them. "If we tied a knot in the fascists' tails in Tulle, this has to be a kick in the teeth."

"What's worse, a knot in the tail or a kick in the teeth?" Geronimo mused, sipping on a bottle of Australian rum.

"Hope it's not the straw that breaks the camel's back," Blackburn raised his eyebrows as he saw a policeman tied to a pillar being pelted with rotten vegetables by a group of children. "My people weren't very happy about what happened when the Nazis retook Tulle. People back home could mistake this whole escapade as bear-baiting at the civilians' expense."

"This is not going to happen," Guevremont assured them. "I have a company of men about two kilometers south of here awaiting the fascists. They will give us enough time to evacuate the civilians."

"You're full of shit," Geronimo cackled. "The Nazis have flamethrowers, they'll incinerate them in the woods. Where else would you take them on short notice? You'll leave them right here and hope they can bullshit their way out of it."

"Plus the fact that we're wise to your game, we've been privy to some of your messages," Blackburn twisted open his own bottle of rum. "You fellows think it's to your advantage for the Nazis to burn everyone in town. The more atrocities they commit, the more we'll pay you to help us wrap this thing up."

"How can you say such a thing?" Guevremont objected. "You're suggesting that we are sacrificing our own people!"

---

2. blue, white and red

"Hey," Geronimo tapped him on the arm. "Stalin has probably killed over a million of his own people already, and we're not talking Jews. We know you Commie bastards hold nothing sacred."

"This is an outrage!" Guevremont stammered.

"I'm sure the Nazis would agree," Blackburn yawned as the three men stopped in the middle of the square. "Okay, I'm bored. What else do you have for us?"

"Madame Natasha. Radio Utopia," Guevremont replied grandly. "We have scheduled a live broadcast from the town hall. The broadcast team is due here within an hour. My men are already setting up the equipment as we speak."

"You getting any?" Geronimo nudged him.

"I beg your pardon!" Guevremont was indignant.

"Yep, he's getting some," Blackburn chuckled. "Look, boyo, we'll be in touch. Don't forget, we're expecting your best at Oradour."

"The Nazis will be late," Guevremont called after them as they headed off towards their limousine outside the square. "They'll be licking their balls for a couple of days after this."

"Good luck," Geronimo raised his bottle to him.

"When can we expect our next payment?" Guevremont called out once more.

"Check's in the mail," Blackburn raised a hand as they walked off.

As they got into the limousine, they were somewhat surprised to see a petite young woman sitting inside waiting for them. They looked quizzically at their chauffeur who held the door open for them.

"She's here under orders from SOE," the chauffeur said quietly.

"You must be…" Blackburn stared.

"Violette Szabo," she exchanged firm handshakes with the agents. "I'm working with Jacques Dufour among the *maquis* here in Limousin."

Violette was a petite, raven-haired woman with piercing eyes, sensuous lips and a captivating personality. She had already become a legend in SOE and along the Resistance underground network in France. Her husband was killed in action against General Rommel's

forces in El Alamein, and she dedicated her life to avenging his death. She was a seasoned parachutist, a crack shot and had a solid reputation as a field strategist and tactician.

"What brings you around these parts?" Geronimo offered her a drink which she declined.

"I'm working with the *maquis* to coordinate our efforts against the Das Reich Division," she revealed. "They asked me to meet with you to find out how things are developing in your negotiations with the FFI. They are very concerned that SOE is going to pave the way for a Communist takeover after the war is over. They want you to understand that they are not fighting this war just to have France become a Communist country."

"It's not what Churchill wants, nor what Baker Street[3] wants," Blackburn assured her. "Look, we're trying to get the FFI off the bench but it takes time. There's as many as ten rival factions under the flag of the Armee Secrete, and De Gaulle is having as much trouble with them as we are. Things are coming along, Violette, rest assured. The Jockey Network under Francis Cammaerts has recruited over 10,000 agents along the Rhone Valley. We've still got the Wrestler and the Prosper Network going as well."

"We're just using the FTP until the FFI's ready to take over," Geronimo insisted. "You'll see. Just tell the *maquis* to hold tight, Patton and Montgomery are going to build a highway straight through France right into Berlin. Keep the faith, it's almost over."

"I'll tell them," her eyes brightened. "I trust you on this, and I know they will too."

They shook hands once more before she took leave.

They could not imagine they would never see her again.

* * *

"Surely you're joking, Jacques! Tell us you're joking!"

Lucien Belmondo and the others stared at Jacques Tremblay as he revealed to them the gist of his conversation with Madame Dominique the previous evening. They were in a safe house courtesy of Pierre Le Blanc, whose patronage they continued to enjoy during their sojourn in Limousin. Le Blanc, in turn, appreciated the generosity of his guests and afforded them limited protection as a chieftain in the *maquis* network.

"Look, I told you that I told her I would talk it over with you fellows, so don't get your shorts bunched up," Jacques bristled. "I'll tell you something, though. We've always bitched and moaned about how we ended up on the wrong side of the law because life gave us the shaft since we were kids in the streets of

---

3. SOE HQ

Paris together. We used to sit in the gutter and look up at the Eiffel Tower and talk about how we were going to take what was ours one day. Well, now they're bringing us our share on a silver platter. They're opening the door and rolling out the red carpet. We'll have jobs in their system, negotiating, bargaining, playing politics, making deals. Only we won't need guns and knives to back us up. Now it'll be the new French government, not the Mob, not anymore."

"I don't know," Jean-Paul Marat ran his fingers through his hair. "We're going to be like a bunch of alley cats in a town house, pissing all over the furniture, fucking the house cats, tearing up the curtains, think about it. I drink a milliliter of cognac in the morning before lunch, I smoke two packs of cigarettes a day, I smoke hash whenever I can get it, and if I can have sex at any given time, everything else has to wait. That bubble will bust for me, Jacques, how could it not?"

"C'mon, guys," Jacques reasoned. "You read the papers. They say that's what brought the Third Republic down. This is what politicians do. They're the same as us, no different deep down. Only we had the guts to steal that shipment when they couldn't protect it. For that, they're offering us the chance to become one of them."

"Ask Le Blanc to reach out for us," Lucien decided. "Tell him we want to hear what Paris has to offer. It won't hurt to see what they have to say."

"Okay," Jacques conceded. "I'll talk to Le Blanc, tell them we want to cut a deal to bring the shipment in. They have to guarantee at least two million francs, plus protection from Henri and his crew. That'll give us enough time to leave the country."

"You don't think those jobs might still be out there?" Marcel wondered.

"You know, Oink, you make me laugh," Jacques used his childhood street name. "Always trying to have your cake and eat it too."

"And doesn't he look it," Lucien reached over and patted Marcel's bulging midsection as Marcel playfully shoved him back. It was one of the few lighter moments they would share together.

Jacques was on the phone with Le Blanc, who, in turn, made a call to his Parisian contacts. It was a touchy political situation as the Lafont Brothers were top lieutenants in the Bony-Lafont Gang, and to circumvent Henri Lafont in such a matter was considered a grave insult. Another problem was that both Pierre Bony and Henri Lafont had been contracted by the Gestapo in Paris as double agents in the Parisian underworld. It provided them with enormous leverage over the entire underground network, second only to that of the Corsican Mob. Anyone coming afoul of Bony or Lafont risked not only retribution from their gang, but also having their name forwarded to the Gestapo as an enemy of the state.

The *maquisard* network in Paris was well-protected by the Unione Corse, and despite the best efforts of Henri Lafont, Le Blanc's contacts were steadfast in refusing to give him up. Lafont was outraged yet realized his only option was to turn the *maquisards* over to the Nazis, which would have resulted in a gang war against the Corsicans. That, he knew, would have led to the annihilation of his entire gang regardless of their status within the Gestapo.

Lafont agreed to have one of his teams meet with the Tremblay Gang to negotiate the return of the morphine and guaranteed their safety at the sitdown. They arranged the meeting at Vierzon, which was due north from Oradour and would ensure the Tremblays relative security within the *maquis* network.

Jacques arrived at the warehouse where the meeting was scheduled just before dawn that morning. He instructed the others to safeguard the morphine and await his call before proceeding. If he used the name 'Oink' at any time, it meant that he had been captured and used as bait for a trap, and Lucien would be deputized to resume negotiations with Henri Lafont.

Jacques parked the borrowed Citroen outside the warehouse and crept quietly towards the darkened entrance, which had been left ajar as agreed. It was a free-standing building with covered parking in adjacent lots that were occupied by some empty trailers. Jacques was confident that he had arrived before the Parisians, and decided to assume a position near a front window to await the negotiators.

"Don't make a move, you piece of shit."

Jacques froze as he perceived four figures surrounding him on each side as he stepped through the warehouse door. He felt a man behind him come up and frisk him, relieving him of his Beretta before shoving him forward.

"Where are your rat friends?" the leader, standing before Jacques, demanded. "Did they leave you die alone?"

"They've got the stuff," Jacques sneered. "If I don't come back they deal direct to the Sicilians. You, the *maquis*, the Resistance and the Nazis all get shit."

"You're going to take us right to them," the leader retorted. "If you don't, I start with your left eye before I take off your fingers."

"Fuck you!" Jacques hawked and spit in his face. The men on either side of him grabbed an arm as the man behind him kicked the back of his knee, dropping him to the ground. His hair was yanked back so that he could see the leader coming forward with a stiletto in his hand.

"Germaine and I go back a long way," the man grinned. "Almost as far as Henri and I. He would've enjoyed this as much as I will."

At once there was a loud thumping noise echoing from the catwalk surrounding the grade level, and the men froze in alarm as the leader's skull exploded in a shower of gristle over Jacques' face. They began drawing their pistols as the silhouette of a man dropped from the catwalk to the concrete floor. Jacques watched as the muzzle flare across the room erupted twice, the chests of the gangsters on either side of him exploding in plumes of blood. The leader, having spun to face the rifleman, was gut shot so that he sprawled in agony to Jacques' left.

"You're making a mistake!" the leader screamed in broken German as the black-clad figure approached. "This bastard is the hijacker from Brive! We were hired to bring him in with the stolen morphine!"

"Bullshit!" Carl Hansen scoffed as he pointed the rifle, fitted with a silencer and a long-range night scope, at the man's face. "Your calls were intercepted by the Gestapo in Paris. You were getting a million francs for killing this scumbag and his men before taking the drugs back to Bony and Lafont, and their Corsican connection."

"He was going to sell the drugs to the Resistance!" the leader pleaded. "He was dealing directly with Madame Dominique! We confirmed it with our *maquis* connections!"

"That's what I needed to know," Carl said before blowing the man's head off.

"Now what?" Jacques grunted, remaining on his knees, staring furtively at the pistols on the ground far from beyond reach.

"I need proof of life," Carl jacked a fresh round into his rifle. "Describe her."

"So you can arrest her? Fuck you."

"There's a man I know whose daughter is missing. He asked me to find out if she was all right. I think she's tied up with the Resistance. You're going to lead me to her eventually, that's why you're still alive. I just need to know it's not a dead end."

"Okay," Jacques' eyes widened as Carl pointed the rifle at his kneecap. "We spoke through a curtain, like a veil, I didn't see her face. She's medium height, about two and a half meters, nice build, long dark hair. All of France knows her voice. That's all I got. Don't you think I would've found her by now if I knew what she looked like?"

"I want you to touch your forehead to the ground and count backwards from one hundred," Carl ordered. "I'll be counting along with you. I can take out a bird from three hundred meters with this rifle. Test me on this, you'll be crippled for life."

Jacques cursed and swore intermittently as he completed the count before gathering the firearms and the dead men's wallets before returning to his Citroen, parked right where he left it. The tires squealed as he peeled out of the lot and back down the road to Limoges.

He would be looking over his shoulder for a long, long time.

Chapter Five

The Leader Regiment rumbled along the way to the quaint little town of Limoges. Despite the tranquility of the mellifluous countryside, the atmosphere surrounding the armored convoy was thick with trepidation. Their radio signals were being jammed, the only transmissions leaking through either those of the underground radio or distress signals from the Vichy forces.

"Another Tulle?" Carl exhaled tautly as he and Heinz Barth rode ahead of the Panzer tank running the point position ahead of the Company convoy. He had napped most of the way following the previous hours' activity and was rested by the time Heinz came within view of the town.

"I hope not," Heinz peered intently through the windshield of the jeep as they made a tight turn along the road to the village. The town limits were within their sight, and Heinz slowed their approach as they looked around for signs of activity.

The commandos slowed to a halt as they saw anti-German and pro-Communist graffiti scrawled across the walls of buildings and windows draped with banners bearing similar messages. Like Tulle, however, the insurgents were long gone by the time the Company arrived. Heinz drove cautiously towards the town square where they parked the jeep and began searching door to door, covering each other in turn.

"The terrorists went into the wind," Carl radioed back to the regimental convoy's point units. "All clear."

At once, bedlam broke out throughout the town as police sirens filled the air. The GMR and the Gestapo flooded the streets with trucks, squad cars, motorcycles and personnel, hammering on doors and issuing directives over bullhorns.

"I think this is what the Americans refer to as coming on like gangbusters," Heinz mused as they watched the civilian population slowly filling the sidewalks, who in turn watched the police action in shock and awe. They both grimaced in dismay as the police began dividing the villagers into groups, men being separated from the women and children.

"What the hell?" Carl growled. "There's nothing going on here, what's this about?"

"I think someone hasn't resolved their Tulle issues," Heinz noted.

"I discussed this with Schweinberg," Carl snapped as Heinz swung the jeep around and began cruising back to the city limits where the regiment was rolling into town. "He said there would be no reprisals as long as there were no German casualties. I haven't risked my life for five years for this division to watch it degenerate into a murder machine. And I'm not being drawn into a murder conspiracy either."

"For a guy with over two hundred registered kills, that is kind of funny," Heinz suppressed a grin.

"Killing enemy in combat is one thing," Carl retorted. "Murdering innocent civilians is another. Rest assured Schweinberg's going to know the difference."

* * *

"I thought we had a deal."

"Damn it, Carl!" Gunter Schweinberg nearly fell out of his chair at his desk in the dimly-lit office at the police station. "How in the hell did you get in here! You scared the crap out of me!"

"You said you were going to keep this under control. Where are the women and children?"

Carl had been sitting in the shadows on a windowsill about six feet from the floor. He jumped down and Gunter could see he wore a black jumpsuit, his sawed-off shotgun strapped to his thigh, Mauser on his hip.

"They're being rounded up at the town square, you know the routine," Gunter composed himself. "There'll be the identification checks, debriefings, interrogations of persons of interest."

"Women of interest," Carl mused. "Children of interest."

"Carl, I don't make the rules. You saw what these people did at Tulle. They executed forty of our soldiers."

"The partisans killed our soldiers, not women and children. What do you call what your death squads did in return? Ninety-nine civilians murdered, none of whom were proven to be combatants."

"It wasn't Einsatzgruppen, it was the Pioneer Platoon, you know that."

"You know what, I'm not standing between you and Eric anymore," Carl stormed towards the door. "You two can go fuck each other."

"I didn't help you because of Eric," Gunter called after him. "I like you, Carl."

Carl turned to stare at him.

"You're a good man. You've restored my faith in the good in people. You risk your life every single day you're here, yet you take it upon yourself to risk even more for others."

"So why don't you try and find some good in yourself?" Carl retorted.

"I've got an idea."

The Einsatzgruppen agents had taken control of the local police station and were rounding up citizens in the town square. After hours of processing, the men were separated from the women and children and taken to a nearby gymnasium. The women and children, frightened, hungry and exhausted, were herded into an enclosed parking area awaiting further instructions.

Carl and Gunter trudged up to the front desk, where the senior officer stood and gave them the Nazi salute.

"We're here to take possession of the female and underage detainees," Gunter informed him.

"I don't understand," the officer was bemused. "You've already sent them back here. Why would you want them up front again?"

"We believe that if we place these people at the front of our convoy as human shields, the insurgents would think twice before they try and attack our soldiers," Gunter explained.

"Excellent idea!" the officer said admiringly. "Maybe that'll keep these frogs out of the way so we can kick the limeys and the Yanks off the beach!"

Carl and Gunter entered the enclosure and confronted the terrified civilians. Children hid in fright behind their mothers' skirts at the sight of Gunter's SS uniform.

"You know, you might avoid going around like it's *Seleenwoche*[1]," Carl taunted him.

---

1. All Souls' Week, or Halloween Week

"What's she saying?" Gunter squinted as a slim young woman spoke French with Carl, glancing furtively towards Gunter.

"She says that the word has spread across the region about the men in black, that they kill all the men and take the women and children away to labor camps. I assured her that you were just a clerk who doesn't know his ass from his elbow."

"Nice, Carl," Gunter looked away.

"Okay, let's go," Carl led him back towards the main building. "Looks like we'll need about three or four trucks."

"Where on earth do you think we'll take them?" Gunter hissed furtively, eyes darting around for eavesdroppers.

"Anywhere but a labor camp or an execution pit," Carl snapped. "I'm doing you a favor. It's bad luck to kill women and children, not to mention the possibility that the Allies could win and charge you for a war crime."

"You're just brimming with optimism, aren't you?"

"I'm a realist, and I just came back from Russia. It's not looking good for the home team."

At length Gunter was on the phone with the local Gestapo HQ, and three trucks arrived in order to transport the civilians to a military interrogation center for debriefing. Gunter and Carl commandeered two of the trucks, dismissing the drivers in doing so. Upon returning to the compound, they recruited an able-bodied matron as a driver in relieving the third Gestapo man. She was instructed by Carl to follow the lead truck, with the other following behind her. She was also warned of the consequences should she attempt to deviate from their course. The civilians boarded the trucks and were delighted to find the baskets of bread and milk that were loaded at Carl's request.

"Where to?" Gunter called over.

"Follow me," Carl climbed into the cab of the lead truck.

They drove for a short distance until arriving at the village of Sussac, about eight kilometers southeast of Limoges. The trucks rumbled into town and idled in the town square until a group of officials from the mayor's office arrived to inquire.

"These people have been evacuated from Limoges by police and military personnel," Carl announced as he hopped down from the truck. "They will need temporary lodging for a couple of days until the emergency is under control. We urge you not to attempt to contact their next of kin until the situation returns to normal. They have been evacuated without notice and their disappearance may be regarded with suspicion by law enforcement officials."

"Are you…SS?" the mayor glanced over at Gunter by the rear truck.

"He's full time, I work weekends," Carl replied. "We'll take two of the trucks, see if you can service the other one, we'll send someone for it in a couple of days."

"Certainly, monsieur," the mayor beamed happily as Carl and Gunter reentered their trucks and proceeded back to Limoges, the women and children cheering and waving as they drove away.

Shortly after the trucks disappeared from view, two figures emerged from the shadows and came to where the mayor and his entourage stood. Commander Staunton of SOE was accompanied by Violette Szabo, who had recently joined his unit. They had been frustrated by the ineptitude of the local FFI forces and were doing the best to coordinate attacks on nearby railways and telephone lines that were days behind schedule.

"Talk about a stroke of luck," Staunton was relieved as they watched the women and children led away to a nearby church. "Thank God that not all the Nazis are murdering devils."

"I think we will have exhausted their patience by tomorrow," Violette replied as they walked with the mayor back to the town hall. "Let's hope that F Section gets our logistics sorted out so we can equip our reinforcements properly."

"Blackburn and Geronimo should be here in the morning," Staunton assured her. "I'm pretty sure that those cash cows will have these farmers lined up with their stools and buckets in short order."

* * *

"You've got a visitor."

"Who is it?"

Carl and Gunter arrived that afternoon, tired from the bumpy and dusty round-trip drive. He headed back to his motel room with a pint of milk and some bread, *brie* and *pate*, and was highly irritated by the knock on the door.

"Some peasant from Montauban," the Einsatzgruppen soldier smirked as he exhaled a stream of cigarette smoke, leaning in the doorway. He saw Carl's expression as he glared at the cigarette and quickly snuffed it in a nearby ashtray.

"What does he want?"

"He says he's a member of the City Council. He says you and his daughter went to school together."

The soldier watched with alacrity as Carl yanked on his clothes and sprinted out the door. He ran down the street to the police station and inquired of the desk officer before being escorted to the room where his visitor awaited.

"Carl."

"Francois."

Carl shook the hand of his visitor, Francois Dagineau, fascinated by the look of the man and how he had aged over the last five years. He managed to hide his wonderment but could not refrain from a tentative embrace. The man's rigidity compelled Carl to reluctantly release him, allowing Carl to recheck his own emotions.

"There's a delightful little cafe down the street," Carl smiled. "I'll buy you coffee."

Shortly thereafter, the two were seated at a corner bistro where they were sipping espresso and nibbling at *pate* on crackers. They studied each others' countenances, nearly distracted by their own trains of thought.

"You've changed, Carl, you've matured," Francois finally spoke. "You're not the boy Angie brought home from the University. I sense that you've found a side of yourself that would have taken you many years to find...were it not for the war."

"How's things at home?" Carl managed a smile. "How's Angie?"

"That's...that's why I'm here," Francois looked down into his cup. "She left home almost a month ago."

"That's impossible! She came to see me in Toulouse."

"She did not come from Montauban. She left home one morning and I haven't seen her since. Carl, I am afraid that she has joined the Resistance."

"Why would you think that?" Carl broke out in a cold sweat.

"We had some long discussions about the war before she left," the older man revealed. "She changed somehow, Carl. She kept on and on about how it was every Frenchman's role to stand up and fight for what was theirs. Some-how...somehow I could not help but think she was talking about you."

"She could be anywhere," Carl crushed his napkin in his fist.

"Paris would be the best bet. There's a strong underground network, it's heavily populated by political activists and intellectuals. They...we...can't control it, it is what it is. It would be the most logical place. Do you have connections in Paris?"

"She's not in Paris," Francois swallowed hard. "Of that I am almost certain."

"It makes no sense," Carl growled. "I saw her just days ago, I know her as well as anyone, I..."

He stared into the older man's eyes.

"I'm going to marry her, Francois. I want you to know that."

"Okay," he lowered his eyes.

"You have no right to judge," Carl insisted. "No one has a right to judge! If I've learned one thing, that is what I've learned. I don't care what you think about me, I've always respected you and I always will. And I will find Angie. And if she is alive I would die before I lose any and all hope of making her my wife."

"I....traveled this distance to hear that," Francois stood up. "I just wanted to know that you still cared."

"You knew I cared," Carl grew angry. "You just wanted to see if I would do something."

"She's all I have, Carl," he wiped a tear from his eye.

"She's all I have, Francois."

The older man returned Carl's embrace before walking from the patio and down the hazy street. Carl continued to gaze at the street long after Francois had disappeared.

Major Helmut Kampfe, according to all accounts, had pushed his luck even farther than Carl Hansen or Robert Ruess ever had.

He has become enchanted by the French countryside and its rustic charm, growing increasingly fonder of its wine, women and song. His good looks and debonair manner made him popular with the females, and his derring-do enhanced his reputation on the field so that he was being compared favorably to Hansen and Ruess. Much like the competition, he was taken to going out his own to troubleshoot problems and, like Ruess, he had gone one time too many.

Kampfe's 3rd Battalion had been bogged down along their route from Limoges to Gueret, which had become a hotbed of insurgent activity. His men had captured and executed twenty-nine *maquisards*, yet the rebels kept attacking. Kampfe, taking matters into his own hands, commandeered a late-model Talbot and informed his point runners that he was going to run recon and take out any insurgents along the way. About an hour later, the Talbot was found alongside the road with its motor still running outside La Bussiere. Kampfe was nowhere to be found.

Gilles Guevremont had retreated from Tulle shortly after the SS arrived and set up shop in the region of Sussac, where he had a battalion of 300 Alsatian Jews at his command. His right-hand man in the region, Jacques Dufour, had been contacted by Commander Staunton at Blackburn and Geronimo's request, and they had arranged a meeting between Violette Szabo and Dufour to coordinate Resistance activity against Das Reich in the area. When Guevremont heard of Kampfe's capture he ordered the Major brought to him immediately, while dispatching Dufour to deal with Violette.

By the time Kampfe was brought to Guevremont at the insurgent campsite on the outskirts of Breuilaufa, he had been beaten to a pulp by the four-man gang that captured him. He was barely conscious and had to be dragged from their vehicle over to Guevremont's tent.

"Well, well," Guevremont chortled. "These Nazi bastards don't look so tough when the shoe's on the other foot, do they? Assemble the men!"

Squad leaders barked orders as the fighters returned from their various chores to gather around the bloodied victim, spitting, cursing and striking him. Finally he was dragged to a small platform from where Guevremont spoke at battalion meetings. Guevremont instructed his men to bring a chair and rope to the platform. They bound Kampfe to the chair as Guevremont brought up a can of petrol.

"They'll have two Skullfaces now," Guevremont laughed as he poured the gasoline over Kampfe's head.

He lit a match and held it until he caught Kampfe's attention. After a long moment he tossed it in Kampfe's face, and his agonized scream was soon drowned out by the cheering roar of his battalion cadre.

"I don't think this one will be opening a torture chamber anytime soon," Guevremont chuckled as he handed the empty can over to one of his men.

They continued cheering until the body of Helmut Kampfe had become a charred, unrecognizable mass.

* * *

Eric Von Hoffman arrived at the chalet along the outskirts of St. Junien just before dark. He was curious as to the Einsatzgruppen soldiers overseeing the property but even more so as to the purpose of the invitation.

A soldier led him upstairs to a master chamber and tapped softly on the door. A command was given to enter and the soldier held the door for Eric before closing it softly behind him.

"Sgt. Von Hoffman," the athletically-built man stood in the shadows, wearing an expensive black silk robe. "May I call you Eric?"

"Why not? Everybody else does."

"Care to join me for a drink?"

"Sure."

"Do you smoke?"

"Sometimes. Not right now."

"Good. Have a seat."

Eric obliged, yet did not even blink as he came face-to-face with the disfigured Captain Ruess. He had cut more than one Russian son of a bitch's face off in his time. He thanked the Captain as he brought Eric a glass of cognac.

"So. It appears that push has come to shove. The insurgents have dealt us tremendous blows."

"I do believe that the Lord's justice shall prevail," Eric grinned.

"Sometimes justice is delayed, for reasons known only to the Almighty himself," Ruess sipped his cognac. "The only reason why I'm still out here commanding troops is to ensure that justice is served."

"I like to think that the reason I'm still alive is to continue doing His work."

"I'm sure you are, Eric," Ruess leaned back in his chair. "You know, I've taken some time to review your dossier. I've learned quite a bit about you. You come from a religious family, like me. You're also a Bavarian like I am. We have so much in common. Sometimes I think if I ever had a son, he'd probably be a lot like you."

"So," Eric chuckled. "Can I call you Dad?"

They stared at one another for a long moment before sharing a laugh.

"Okay, let's get down to business," Ruess patted his leaking face with a handkerchief. "I had one of my informants approach Major Diekmann this evening with information that Major Kampfe was abducted by terrorists earlier today."

"Is that a fact?"

"Diekmann's checking it out as best he can. I'm sure you're well aware of the fact that Diekmann's got an in with Reichsfuhrer Himmler. Plus the fact that Diekmann and Kampfe are asshole buddies. I think Diekmann's got people sniffing around before he makes his move tomorrow. He's going in hard and fast, and he wants to make sure he's on solid ground in case this draws down more heat than Tulle. He's called a staff meeting for tomorrow morning, and they'll probably hit Oradour sometime after noon."

"Sounds like fun," Eric chuckled.

"Here's what's going down," Ruess folded his hands. "There are two Oradours, Oradour-sur-Glane and Oradour-sur-Vayres. I've got reason to suspect that Carl Hansen has been collaborating with Gunter Schweinberg to rescue the women and children in the insurgent areas along the way to Normandy. I think he'll try to minimize the damage Diekmann may be planning on inflicting. Now, Oradour-sur-Vayres is a major stronghold within the Resistance network. If Diekmann hits that target, it could prove highly embarrassing if we are tied up there for longer than necessary. On the other hand, Oradour-sur-Glane is a much softer target. We can make it a major example to the insurgents and the indigenous population, plus…other things."

"Like what?"

"I have information that the village is used by the insurgents as a major vehicle depot. In this economy, petrol is liquid gold. They're also manufacturing uniforms there for the French Army if the Allies ever break through. I think the rebels are using Glane as a supply base for Vayres. I think it may be of great help to the war effort if we…confiscate their resources."

"Sounds like a lot of moving, Captain. I'm not sure I can loot a whole town by myself."

"I'm sending you with five of my men," Ruess shoved a sealed envelope across the table to Eric. "You'll open this tomorrow morning and go over your instructions carefully. I have an informant meeting with Hansen tomorrow morning. He will be sending Hansen to the wrong Oradour. Hansen'll take his sergeants, but you won't be there. Once he leaves, you'll report to Lt. Barth and tell him Hansen assigned you to his unit. When you get there, you'll follow your instructions to the letter."

"I'm getting the feeling," Eric drained his glass as Ruess reached over to refill it, "that this is going to be a real interesting assignment."

"It will," Ruess grinned. "This is a chance for you to really get to play God."

"I'm starting to like this job already."

They shared yet another hearty laugh.

Colonel Stadler called an emergency meeting of his staff at daybreak on the morning of June 10, 1944. The Gestapo had reported that Major Kampfe's identity papers were found in an alleyway in Limoges, whereupon Major Diekmann revealed that he had been given information by a couple of villagers from Sussac that a German officer was being held prisoner by the *maquis* at Oradour.

"They came to my villa about a half hour ago with the information!" Diekmann exclaimed. "We've got to move quick on this. The bastards captured Captain Gerlach and his driver last night and stripped them to their underwear before taking them to Oradour. Gerlach escaped, but God knows what happened to his driver."

"This is unbelievable," Stadler murmured, running his fingers through his hair. "As if we don't have enough to deal with at Normandy. Gentlemen, we have to crush these bastards before we lose control of the entire region."

"Let me try and make a deal with the terrorists," Diekmann entreated him. "If we offer a ransom or a prisoner exchange we may be able to save him."

"You can't negotiate with terrorists," Carl insisted. "They have no rules, no Geneva Convention to abide by. These are war criminals and have to be dealt with accordingly. If you release criminals and send them money there's nothing to stop them from killing the Major anyway."

"We can't take that chance, Colonel," Diekmann snapped.

"All right, Adolf," Stadler relented. "I'll give the SD^2 a call and make sure you've got their full cooperation. The rest of you, instruct your men that these terrorists have to be stopped at all costs. There's too much at stake in Normandy for us to be losing men and material in this shithole!"

Carl trotted back to his motel where his team leaders were billeted. He called his sergeants to his room for a meeting, and Beckmann, Garthaffner and Tollner arrived within minutes. Von Hoffman was nowhere to be found.

"Stupid bastard," Carl hissed as his men took seats around the small room. "Has anyone seen him?"

"He got a visit last night from one of Ruess' Einsatzgruppen men," Beckmann informed him. "I'm not sure if he got back. Do you think he got kidnapped too?"

---

2. SS Intelligence

"The terrorists don't have anyone who could handle Eric," Carl retorted. "I knew Ruess had his own agenda out here, that bastard. He's using his connections to get Eric to do a job for him."

"Want us to get someone from Barth's platoon?" Tollner asked.

"Barth's men'll be going out with Diekmann," Carl growled.

"Diekmann thinks he'll be able to make a deal for Helmut, which isn't going to happen. There's a small town near here called Gueret that may be standing by to get wiped out. If we can get over there and then to Oradour before Diekmann we may be able to convince them to evacuate the women and children."

"Won't we be tipping off the terrorists?" Garthaffner was concerned.

"Are you kidding?" Carl scoffed. "We're like King Kong out here, we lift our toe and the trees start shaking. Besides, Diekmann will be coming with everything he has, and if the terrorists haven't hit the road by then, they damned sure will be."

Carl arrived at the small town with Hans Beckmann, Peter Garthaffner and Michael Tollner shortly after 0900 on the morning of June 10, 1944. They rode their motorcycles into the town square and parked them as the villagers began to gather in wonderment.

"Do you speak French?" an elderly man approached them. "I am the mayor. Welcome to Gueret."

"We have reason to believe your town may be in danger," Carl spoke excellent French. "A German officer has been murdered and it is believed that the assassins are in hiding in this region of Limousin. There is a standing policy of swift reprisal in effect, and we have come to escort your women and children to safety."

"Where...where will they go?" the mayor's voice grew husky. "What shall we do?"

"Do as we tell you," Carl ordered. "Have every available vehicle brought to the town square, from trucks to bicycles. Have all the women and children bring a change of clothing, food and water, make sure they are carrying as little as possible, no more than a sack or a basket. We will get you moving south to where the *maquis* can ensure safe passage to the Spanish border."

"Spain," the mayor considered. "What will they have in Spain?"

"They will live," Carl insisted.

"And maybe you will not," a voice called.

The commandos stared apprehensively as over two dozen riflemen stepped away from their positions in the buildings surrounding the square. Carl cursed and swore in realizing the folly of not having heeded Gunter's warning that Gueret was considered a *Maquis* stronghold.

"We're done, Carl," Peter swallowed hard, leveling his rifle as they stood back-to-back facing in each direction. "They'll take us like they've taken the others."

"You know who we're with," Carl's voice boomed out. "You know who we are. We can't stop our army from coming for revenge, but we can help you save the innocent. We were able to save the children of Limoges just as we can save yours."

"I've heard of you," the leader stepped forth, lowering his rifle though none of his men did so. "I know what you've done. I also know what your murderous bastards have done before and after you. Why do you do this?"

"What are they saying?" Hans hissed.

"I don't know," Michael replied anxiously. "I don't think they like us."

"We don't believe in killing women and children. Our fight is with the Allies, not with you. If you take it upon yourselves to stand against us, so be it. Just don't allow your women and children to be caught in the middle."

"Let's wipe the scum out," a man behind him snarled.

"Dufour," another man called out. "We're getting a field transmission on the radio. The Nazis are moving towards Oradour-sur-Glane."

"Oradour-sur-Glane," Carl muttered in disbelief. At once he realized that Ruess was behind it all. He wanted to make sure that Carl could not interfere...and that Eric was with Heinz and Captain Kahn when Diekmann came for his revenge.

Eric.

"All right," the *maquis* leader relented. "Assemble the women and children and have them placed on trucks and driven south. We will allow these fellows safe passage back to town."

"I say we hang the Nazi bastards," a rebel snarled in the background to a chorus of assenting voices.

"Get ready," Carl tensed his muscles, ready to explode into action. His men prepared to aim and fire on command.

"These men risked their lives to come here and warn us to protect our women and children," the leader shot back. "Are we cowards and backstabbers that we would reward this gesture with treachery? Go in peace, and tell your leaders that we will be waiting."

"Hopefully we'll find better things to do," Carl said as the commandos mounted their bikes and began cruising back to Limoges.

Little did they know that their race against time was just beginning.

Chapter Six

Jacques Tremblay and his gang stepped off the tram at the station at Oradour-sur-Glane, a sightseeing resort conveniently located along the Glane River just six kilometers from Limoges. Jacques savored the sweet summer breeze wafting from the countryside, enjoying the diversion from their perilous journey throughout Limousin as were his teammates. He was scheduled to call Madame Dominique that evening, and decided to place the call here instead of risk detection in Limoges where Der Fuhrer Regiment was stationed.

The gangsters strolled down the street from the tram station to the Avril Hotel, where crowds of tourists from as far as Paris, Reims and Bordeaux had come to enjoy the town's summer recreational activities. They managed to check in but grew tired of the bustling lobby and opted for lunch at the nearby Milord Hotel. To their chagrin, it was just as crowded, and they finally got a table after a short wait.

"What are all these kids doing here?" Jacques motioned to the large groups of school children romping around the streets outside the hotel.

"The monthly medical checkup is scheduled for today," their waiter informed them. "We have had families evacuated here from Nice, Avignon, Montpelier and Bordeaux, as well as some from Alsace-Lorraine. I understand there are almost two hundred children attending our schools. We've also got a big turnout for tobacco rations and the farmers' market."

"What in hell is that?"

"Time to go," Jacques told the others. "Let's catch the next train out of here. I have a bad feeling it may be the last one."

The squad sergeant leading the forward point units into Oradour-sur-Glane were alerted by the sight of a burned-out ambulance along the side of the road just outside the city limits. They spread out and approached the truck, and were revolted by the sight of two medics and four wounded soldiers who had been burned alive in the ambulance. The driver and his passenger had been chained to the steering wheel. The sergeant radioed back to the command vehicle and reported their grisly findings.

"That's the last straw," Adolf Diekmann snarled. "All right, men, move in!"

Major Diekmann's 1st Battalion surrounded the village of Oradour-sur-Glane by 1400 that afternoon. Diekmann ordered Captain Kahn to deploy two halftracks carrying a squad apiece into

town in order to assemble the residents at the town square. They were instructed to have their identity papers ready upon arrival. Kahn, leading the raid by default in Ruess' absence, left Heinz Barth in charge of the operation.

Earlier that morning, Diekmann had released an insurgent from custody in Limoges to make an offer to the FTP. He proposed the release of a number of suspects being held in Limoges along with a ransom of 40,000 francs in exchange for the safe return of Major Kampfe. When the emissary called back two hours later with no word from the insurgents, Diekmann ordered the battalion to move in on Oradour.

"Why in hell is Von Hoffman here?" Barth asked angrily, noticing Eric and a squad of Einsatzgruppen following his halftracks in a small truck. "He's under Hansen. I'm not going to baby-sit him while we're looking for a gang of armed assassins."

"You may be glad you had him when this is over," Kahn shot back as he returned to his command position along the edge of town. Eric parked the truck and proceeded through the alleys and backroads of the sleepy village, accompanied by the twelve Einsatzgruppen riflemen dispatched by Captain Ruess. They watched in the shadows as the men, women and children slowly assembled in the town square. Heinz was in the middle of the square supervising his men as they checked the papers of each individual. As the search drew to an end, Eric approached Heinz.

"See this?" Eric grinned crookedly, handing Heinz an official document bearing an SS stamp along with an unfamiliar arcane emblem. "I got this from old Skullface, Robert Ruess. It says here that I'm going to take charge of this operation."

"Are you out of your fucking mind?" Heinz exploded in disbelief.

"You see this thing right there?" Eric pointed at the arcane emblem. "This is ODESSA. You heard of them, haven't you?"

"Eric," Heinz cleared his throat, "they'll kill you if you faked this. The Fuhrer himself couldn't save you."

"Tell you the truth," Eric chortled, "I think old Skullface is one of them. Of course, I can't prove anything, but you know what they say about them Werewolves."

"This is deep shit, Eric. There's no such thing as Werewolves."

"I know that, and you know that, but they don't know that. So why don't you go on and get your boys together for some heavy lifting?"

"What do you mean?"

"This paper says that all valuable materials and goods worth transporting are to be loaded up and driven to a destination to be specified forthwith," Eric perused the letter. "Matter of fact, I'm going to give you the letter to show to Diekmann. That will get you to where you need to go, and get you out of my way so I can do what I need to do."

"I'm not getting involved in any of this shit," Heinz shot back.

"Hell, you think Skullface won't court-martial you?" Eric laughed. "Tell you what. There's a row of barns along the edge of town there. You have your platoon round up all the villagers at the fairground so we can do an ID check. Once they get there, you have your boys take the menfolk over to the barns, we'll take it from there. You just have them stand by and do what they're told."

"Fine," Heinz shot back. "I'm putting both squads under your command. I'm going back to secure the perimeter. I don't know what's going on in that sick mind of yours, but just remember OKW isn't going to tolerate another Tulle."

"I'm only obeying orders," Eric handed him the letter. "You better do the same."

"Fuck you," Heinz snarled as he stalked off, leaving Eric Von Hoffman in complete control of Oradour-sur-Glane.

Carl, Hans, Peter and Michael raced their choppers up the road. They reached Oradour-sur-Vayres within a half hour. Carl's logic was that Diekmann would realize they had hit the wrong target and would most likely be at least an hour behind schedule. It would give him time to clear the non-combatants from the field.

About five hours earlier, shortly after Carl and his men had left Gueret, section leader Jacques Dufour had met with Violette Szabo in an effort to coordinate FTP and FFI operations with the *maquis* in the area. Dufour had been ordered by Gilles Guevremont to bring Violette to FTP headquarters in Pompadour, about fifteen kilometers south of Sussac. From there she would be brought to a meeting with Guevremont.

Violette had grown increasingly uncomfortable with Dufour's agenda. The trip to Pompadour was not part of the original plan, neither was the meeting with Guevremont. When Dufour slowed the vehicle to offer a ride to a young boy he recognized along the road, Violette's female instincts took over. She insisted that they stop in Salon-la-Tour in order to call F Section for further instructions. As they did so, they drove directly into a squad of grenadiers from the 1st Battalion of the Deutschland Regiment. Following a shootout, Dufour managed to escape though Violette was captured.

"Well, isn't this my lucky day," Jacques Dufour confronted the bikers as they rolled into town. He was braced by a dozen riflemen, the entourage crossing the town square to meet the soldiers. "Everything comes to he who waits."

They watched anxiously as the bikers positioned their rifles in their laps. Behind them, Carl could see the villagers huddling in doorways in the background, fearful of what was about to transpire.

"I know your network, and how news travels like wildfire out here!" Carl called out. "You know who we are, we've tried to help the people of Gueret and Limoges! We want to help you! Your women and children have no business on the field, we're asking you to move them out of harm's way!"

"You're right, our women and children should not be involved," Dufour walked to where Carl stood, lowering his rifle in response. Dufour, unlike Guevremont, had a reputation for compassion among his people. The capture of Violette was also beginning to weigh heavily on his conscience. "What do you propose?"

"Your men can help them cross over the Spanish border," Carl insisted as both the *maquis* and the commandos slowly lowered their weapons. "Regardless of how this turns out, there will be bloody warfare throughout the area, and there will be reprisals. If we win, you know that there will be SS men wanting revenge against those who killed our fellow soldiers. If we lose, we'll be fighting the Allies every step in our retreat, and they'll be throwing everything they have to try and stop us. Plus we'll be doing everything in our power to stop them. Your women and children must be spared these ordeals."

"How can you help?" Dufour asked.

"We know the areas that have been reconnoitered on our maps," Carl revealed. "They're not going to risk our vehicles on uncharted ground. We can direct the women and children through to the border."

"All right," Dufour exhaled. "Let's get on with it."

* * *

Eric watched as his men directed Barth's squads in herding the male villagers towards the fields along the edge of town. There were six barns situated along the fields, and Eric had his men divide the villagers, one hundred ninety in all, into six groups. He called in six jeeps and ordered the occupants to join Barth's squads in searching the town for contraband.

"Line those bastards up against those barns, hands against the wall, heads down, don't let them see what you're doing," Eric ordered the Einsatzgruppen sergeant, an Alsatian, in command. "Then get those machine guns off those jeeps, we want one in each barn."

"For what?" the Alsatian asked.

"Now, you got eleven men under you, and you think you're going to hold off a hundred and ninety frogs if they come at you?" Eric scoffed at him. "You go do as I said!"

"Sgt. Von Hoffman," Eric received a transmission from one of Barth's sergeants. "We're coming across a bunch of vehicles in the garages and warehouses off the town square. It checks with our intelligence about the terrorists using this place for vehicle storage."

"Good for you," Eric replied. "Now, here's what I want. You get two men for each vehicle and send the others back. You call me back and let me know how many men that leaves you with. You're in charge from here on, you report to me directly. I want you to get all the vehicles out on the street."

The Alsatian returned and reported that the machine guns were in the barns. Eric instructed him to have the detainees sent inside and spread-eagled under guard. He then hopped into a nearby jeep and drove with the man towards the barn farthest along the row.

"Well, let's go on in and get the party started," Eric hopped from the truck. The Alsatian followed Eric into the barn, watching as he signaled the machine gunner inside to step away from the weapon. He then sat on the soapbox behind the weapon and opened fire, chopping the entire row of men down at the knees.

He led them to the next barn and repeated the process, going on until he had crippled nearly two hundred men.

"Okay," Eric called his men together as they stood in front of the last barn, the groans of the wounded men filling the air. "I want you to go in there and stomp around on those kneecaps. I need you to find out where the gold is."

"Gold?" they exclaimed.

"Old Skullface thinks that one of our convoys that got hit outside Limoges was carrying a shipment of gold bars on its way out of the country. He thinks this is where the rebels are keeping their valuables. Now, I basically don't give a shit myself, I just want to watch frogs die. However, I want you to take your time, grind down as many busted kneecaps as you can, and find out if there's any gold in those hills. I'll give you about fifteen minutes."

Just then the remnant of Barth's platoon trotted up, having parked the vehicles outside the industrial strip as ordered.

"Now, you have those men move all the women and children to the church along the way," Eric instructed the Alsatian. "Give your men about fifteen minutes to collect some intelligence before you send them over to the warehouses. I want everything of value loaded into the vehicles. First make sure those soldiers get the civilians in the church, then you have your boys relieve them so we can have them load those trucks."

"Done," the Alsatian replied as they ordered the soldiers away.

"We have orders from Lt. Barth..." a corporal began.

"Lt. Barth is out there on the city limits drinking lemonade," Eric snapped at them. "I'm in charge here. I want you sons-of-bitches to round up the women and children out there by the fairground and get them inside the church. I'll be there in about twenty minutes. You screw this up and I'll see to it that Diekmann court-martials every one of you."

"Yes, sir," the corporal muttered. He ordered his men to follow him as he ran towards the fairground to continue their mission.

Carl and his men were surrounded by the FTP riflemen as they walked towards the town hall where the women and children of the village were assembled. Many of the women jeered and cursed at the soldiers as they drew near.

"You're not very popular here," Dufour said lightly. "Most of them are wondering why we haven't already burned you alive."

Almost as if on cue, a woman rushed from the crowd with a revolver in hand, pointing it in Carl's face. He held his hands away from his sides as his men unlooped their rifles and aimed them at the woman. The FTP riflemen looked to Dufour for a signal.

"If that bitch shoots, she dies next!" Hans swore.

"You Nazi bastard!" the woman cried in a rage. "My sister was murdered by German scum in Cressac! She was arrested and executed for bringing food to the Jews hiding along the countryside! If she deserved to die for that, then that's all the more reason to kill you!"

"I understand," Carl replied in French, catching the woman unawares as she had not heard him speaking with Dufour. He motioned for his men to lower their arms, though they would not do so. "I only ask that my woman is told that I died helping her people."

"A Frenchwoman?" the woman demanded, face reflecting her uncertainty. "Who is she, you liar!"

"Angelique Dagineau of Montauban."

"A Dagineau of Montauban!" she exclaimed in disdain. "Do you take us for fools! Did you get the idea from a wine bottle!"

"Mademoiselle," Dufour said quietly. "We do know that Francois Dagineau was in Limoges. He made a sizeable contribution to the FFI before leaving. We also know he has been looking for his daughter Angelique."

"What are they saying?" Peter asked his partners.

"I don't speak frog," Michael replied tautly. "I'm shooting that bitch. One of you be sure and take out Dufour."

"How do we know you do not have her in one of your jails, or torture chambers!" the woman exclaimed.

"You don't," Carl said calmly.

The woman eventually lowered her pistol and dissolved into tears. One of Dufour's men came over and gently relieved her of her weapon, leading her away to a nearby storefront.

"You Nazis do have a powerful effect on people," Dufour noted dourly.

"We've done fairly well in the general elections," Carl said airily.

* * *

"Major," Lt. Barth reported to Diekmann at his tent on Masset Farm about a half kilometer outside the city limits, a few kilometers past the village of Bordes. "My men are reporting back from the village. They're being dismissed in small

95

groups by Von Hoffman. I'm not sure what he's doing in there but he's with that bunch of Einsatzgruppen soldiers that have been retained by Captain Ruess."

"Have one of your men get him on the radio," Captain Kahn walked over to where they were from his canvas chair outside the command post. "I'm still not sure why Hansen sent him over."

"Hansen didn't send him over, I'm quite sure," Barth replied.

"Major Diekmann," one of the sergeants approached the tent.

"This note was sent back by Sgt. Von Hoffman."

Diekmann opened the note written on a torn piece of wrapping paper. It read:

BAKERY

"What in the hell?" Diekmann demanded.

"It was taken from a captured terrorist," the sergeant reported.

"The Sergeant thought it was imperative that it be brought to you."

"Bring me a motorcycle and a sidecar," Diekmann ordered. "I want you to take me directly to this bakery!"

"Yes sir," the sergeant rushed away.

Upon arrival at Compain's Bakery, Diekmann and his driver dislodged to find the front door ajar. As they entered, the sickly sweet odor of charred flesh made them both slightly queasy. Diekmann motioned to his driver and the man went behind the counter and pulled the over door open. They were both startled by the sight of a man's corpse inside. As Diekmann looked around the store, he noticed an object on the counter that sent a chill down his spine.

"It's Helmut's Knight's Cross," he was aghast. "The rotten bastards!"

They had no way of knowing that, according to Eric's orders, Compain was shot by one of the Einsatzgruppen men and his body shoved in the furnace. Ruess had given Eric a Knight's Cross to be laid near the corpse should such an opportunity as this arose.

"Sir," his driver pleaded, "you may be in danger here. Our men have complete control of the village. Let me get you back to the perimeter!"

The driver escorted Diekmann back to the chopper and whisked him back up the street and back on the road to the farm property. Diekmann bounded from the sidecar and was beside himself with rage as he told Kahn and Barth what he had found.

"There will be blood," Heinz snarled. The Mayor of Oradour, Dr. Paul Desourteaux, who had been brought to the command post to consult with the battalion leaders, felt a sudden rush of panic but said nothing. His family was among the founders of the village and, in fact, had a street named after one of their forefathers, the Rue Emile-Desourteaux. He had offered himself and his family as hostages but the offer was rejected by Diekmann.

Back in the village, Eric and his riflemen arrived to relieve Barth's troops, who had finished rounding up the women and children at the fairground and were marching them towards the church.

"Monsieur," a woman entreated him in broken German. "I am a former resident of Moselle, I was evacuated from our family property a few years ago. We are staying with relatives in Limoges, we took the tram here to spend the weekend and my husband went to purchase tobacco with his ration card. He has a heart condition, can I go to see if he is all right?"

"I'm sure he'll be just fine," Eric reassured her. "As a matter of fact, I'm sending my men down there directly to make sure everyone's got everything they need while we're finishing the identity check. I'll have some cookies and lemonade brought here as soon as everyone's in the church."

"Bless you," the woman said gratefully as she joined the end of the line. The summer heat was sweltering as the sun blazed down on the village.

"Okay," Eric called the Alsatian over. "You get your men back down and make sure those dumbasses are done loading those trucks. Soon as they're done, get them out of here. I then want you to go back to the barns and put some firewood in the doorways so the frogs can't get out."

"What about these people?" the Alsatian asked.

"You're going to help me tend to that," Eric winked.

Carl and his men watched as the last of the vehicles were loaded with passengers and directed into the queue joining the convoy headed into the countryside due south. The commandos mounted their bikes and took the lead, hoping that they would not be spotted by a random reconnaissance plane or a patrol unit.

At length they reached an obscure dirt road leading to a sharp incline into a valley that appeared to lead into a hilly region due south of Oradour.

"How do we know this isn't a trap!" a rifleman demanded as Dufour exited the lead vehicle to inspect their surroundings before proceeding. "If we take those trucks down there, there would be no chance of escaping if the Nazis show up. That is, if they are not already down there awaiting us!"

"Don't be fools!" Carl growled. "What would've stopped us from having an aircraft or a tank fire on the village? We have no gain in mass slaughter. My division is retaliating for acts of terrorism in this area, and we are risking a court martial coming out here to help your women and children escape! Now, I've told you that our cartographers have not charted this area. If you've got any better ideas, indulge yourselves. Just remember that you were warned."

"I don't know why you're doing this," Dufour said grudgingly, "but I believe you're telling us the truth. Let's get moving."

Carl and his men watched the convoy disappear into the tree-shrouded valley before turning their bikes around and heading back to Limoges.

Before Barth's soldiers had returned to the perimeter, they reported a large cache of petrol cans stored in one of the garages. Eric radioed Diekmann, and it was their consensus that it was

undoubtedly for the use of terrorists in the region. Eric ordered his men to haul the gas cans out of the garage and redistribute them near the barns and the shops along the main street.

"All right, Diekmann's going to want us to torch this place!" Eric ordered. "Dump the cans out in the doorways and light them up!"

"Very well," the Alsatian headed back to where his men awaited further orders. He was going to remind Eric that the men in the barns were still alive, but after the mass murders the Einsatzgruppen had committed throughout Eastern Europe and Russia, this was nothing new. He was somewhat taken aback that this was being done here in France, but orders were orders.

Within minutes, the barns along the edge of town were ablaze, the screams of the men inside muted by the roaring flames and cracking timbers. The soldiers then raced back to the village and began setting the buildings on fire.

Unknown to them, some of the victims of the shooting had managed to crawl free of the burning buildings despite their gunshot wounds. At least one of them had played possum and was able to race away from the scene of the fire.

The man, an Alsatian Jew, was in town for a meeting with a local *maquis* leader when the battalion rounded the men up on the fairgrounds. He was certain that he would be discovered during the identity check, but the soldiers had barely glanced at his papers before sending him to the barns. At that point he was certain they would be killed as had so many of his fellow Jews who had been transported to killing grounds in Eastern Europe.

He knew that his only hope was to pretend he had been shot in the barn, and he writhed on the ground until the soldiers set it on fire. He waited until they retreated before he rushed past the wounded men crawling towards the flaming piles of wood in the doorway. Rushing around to the rear of the barn, he saw that they had set all the other barns on fire as well. He darted furtively back towards town, and realized that they had proceeded to set the residential section and the shops on fire.

His mind and body were racing as he coursed through the back yards of the burning buildings, wondering how he would survive this ordeal. As he ran, he remembered that the *maquis* had stored a large supply of weapons and ammo in the steeple of the local church. He decided that he might be able to sneak into the church and snatch some weapons as he made his escape.

Upon reaching the church, he saw Eric and his men standing out in front, and figured that the SS men were most likely in process of looting the church. He suddenly realized that there was a chance of turning the tables on the marauders.

He snatched a burning piece of wood from a nearby building and rushed towards the rear of the church. He saw a rear window in an upper room, and tossed the torch with all his might. He was elated to watch the wood crash through the window and fall inside. With that, he ran for his life into the tree-line leading to the countryside. He slowed as he saw the cordon of armored trucks and soldiers around the village, and crept into the bushes where he would wait until dark.

Out in front of the church, Eric and his men were plotting their next move when, at once, a deafening explosion rocked the area as the steeple erupted into smoke and flames.

"What in the hell!" Eric marveled. Within moments he could hear the screams and cries of the women and children inside as they pounded at the doors. Eric had instructed his men to barricade the church so no one could escape. His men looked at each other but said nothing.

"Well, it sure looks like the Lord has taken His vengeance without you fellows having to get your hands dirty," he chortled. "Come on, let's get those trucks on the road and the hell out of here. Follow me, I'll get us through the cordon."

"The church is jam-packed with people," the Alsatian pointed out. "If the ones in the rear push hard enough they will force the ones in front through the door, we've seen this before."

"Well, then, move them back," Eric told him. The soldiers proceeded to open fire on the doors, and after more screams and cries, the hammering on the doors was abated.

He and his men trotted back to the heavily-laden vehicles, each taking the wheel of all thirteen. They followed Eric as he was waved through the cordon without incident. Only they took a dirt road into the countryside rather than the highway back to Limoges. At length they came to a secluded clearing where a truck and a travel car were parked. Eric ordered the men to exit the vehicles a short distance away and follow him in the truck as he drove the car back to town.

He rushed to the Citroen and hopped in, gunning the engine and lurching up the road. He watched in his rearview mirror as the Alsatian, at the wheel, turned the ignition key just before the truck exploded in a roar of flames.

Dead men tell no tales, thought Eric.

He drove along the road whistling a Mozart tune...

...closing the chapter on the darkest day in the history of the Das Reich Division.

Chapter Seven

On the following day of Sunday, June 11, 1944, news of what would be forever known as the Oradour Massacre came to light. Six hundred and forty two men, women and children were killed in a matter of hours. The Oradour Catholic Church, with an official capacity of three hundred fifty, had been packed with two hundred forty five women and two hundred seven children.

One woman, a 47-year-old grandmother, Marguerite Rouffanche, was hit five times by the shots fired through the door, yet managed to crawl behind the altar where she found a ladder used for candle lighting. She climbed to a broken window three meters from the ground and hurtled to safety, hiding in a garden behind the presbytery where she remained hidden until the next day. She was brought to Limoges by the *maquis* and gave a full account of the destruction of the Church and the killing of the innocents.

The FFI was experiencing a revival in the area due to the efforts of F Section, particularly the leadership provided by Violette Szabo and the funding of Blackburn and Geronimo. They had no knowledge of an arsenal cache in the church steeple, reflected by a statement issued by Colonel Rousselier, the commander of the 12th military region of the FFI at Limoges. He insisted that there were no military operations scheduled anywhere in the vicinity of Oradour, and that they had neither camps nor arms caches anywhere near the village. This cast the shadow of doubt on the FTP, who continued to deny any responsibility for incidents leading to the tragedy.

The outrage of the French people barely exceeded that of OKW. Field Marshal Erwin Rommel, one of the most chivalrous figures in German military history, was filled with righteous indignation and contacted General Lammerding directly before demanding an inquiry by the Reich Chancellory. Lammerding, in turn, called Colonel Stadler on the carpet and ordered a full investigation into the incident. Stadler, realizing his own career could well be at stake, would make sure that Major Diekmann and those responsible would suffer the full consequences of their actions.

The ODESSA cover-up would act to shroud much of the controversy in mystery for generations to come. The story of the missing SS gold could never be proven or disproven. The plunder from the town also seemed to have disappeared. The *maquis* denied the SS report that the explosion at the church was caused by the hidden weapons arsenal in the steeple, though investigators found that the heat of the blaze was so great that it partially melted the bronze church bell. The *maquis* would later say that the Nazis had planted explosives which they set off by hurling a smoke bomb in the church. This was dismissed by investigators as highly implausible. The people of the village of Oradour would forever remember the massacre. The ruins of the buildings would remain as monuments to the chaos and insanity that reigned on that tragic day.

The effect of the overkill shocked the insurgent network into inactivity following the event. The Resistance leaders of both the FFI and the FTP urged all its members to observe a temporary ceasefire to allow the Das Reich Division passage into Normandy where they would surely be annihilated by the Allied Expeditionary Force. The people of Southern France had suffered grievous loss and could not be allowed to endure any more.

The ensuing police action, however, added insult to injury and served to worsen the ordeal for the inhabitants throughout the region. Klaus Barbie in Lyon ordered the Gestapo and the GMR to implement a full-scale manhunt for insurgent leaders in the area, and all suspected or known terrorists in Southern France were to be extradited directly to Lyon for interrogation. Yet, though the indigenous population was greatly distressed by the police actions, there was a significant percentage of French citizens who felt as if justice was being served.

Although it did not have the same magical mystery connotation that the concept of the Reich[1] had for the German people, the Third Republic had a majesty for many Frenchmen, with a legacy that went as far back as the collapse of the French Empire of Napoleon III in 1870. Out of the ashes rose the Republic, and for better or worse, it endured until the Nazi Invasion and the establishment of the provisional Vichy Government.

---

1. Kingdom

Many Frenchmen blamed the fall of France on the corruption and moral turpitude of the Republic, though conservatives saw the relative leniency of the Reich towards the occupied Northern Territory as a portent of better days to come. Republicans welcomed the opportunities that Vichy offered to those who wished to work for an increasingly improved dialogue between France and the Reich. Reactionaries saw the changing political climate as an opportunity to crush the forces of Communism that threatened French society and culture, its race, religion and nation. They joined the GMR and the Waffen SS in droves.

For conservatives, news of the capture of insurgents was met with mixed emotions. Although the arrest and murder of Jean Moulin was considered a national tragedy by many, the casualties among Alsatian Jewish refugees of the FTP were not a major concern. However, when names in the news included those of FFI operatives, the Republicans could not help but think that the day of liberation had drifted that much further away.

So it was when the names of those captured in the Oradour counterterrorist action were made known to the public. The Vichy press announced the capture of Violette Szabo in Oradour and her pending extradition to Lyon. This, however, was eclipsed by an exclusive report that Madame Natasha had been arrested in the Limousin region near Oradour and was also being extradited to face charges of sedition in Lyon. It caused an even greater shock effect throughout the Resistance network, and both F Section and their OSS counterparts agreed that operations would be suspended until the Nazis began their troop withdrawal from Normandy.

Carl and the men returned to their motel in Limoges on the evening of June 10th in a state of exhaustion. The ride from Oradour had been long and arduous, and they were forced to make numerous detours in order to avoid Diekmann's convoy on the way back along the highway to Limoges. They had rode and walked the motorbikes through numerous fields, ravines and swamps, and were bone-tired at the end of their long trek.

Gunter came out to meet with Carl as the rest of his men headed for their rooms. Carl told him of the success of their mission, and Gunter suggested they head over to the police station to check on the latest developments. The SS and Gestapo had launched a massive manhunt throughout the region, and Carl expressed concern that there might be other villages where the citizens might be endangered by the dragnet.

"You've got an interesting guest," an Einsatzgruppen sergeant greeted Gunter upon their arrival. "She arrived here shortly after you left. She's not very talkative, we thought we'd leave it to you."

Carl and Gunter were led to the basement area of the police station and down a long corridor to an interrogation room at the end of the hall. They were greeted by two SS men who greeted them with the Nazi salute and opened the cell door to permit the entrance.

The white-washed room was barren save for a small table, two chairs and a cot against the far wall, a naked bulb dangling from the ceiling. The prisoner, a petite young woman, cringed at their approach as she laid on the cot. She was clad in a torn blouse and a denim skirt, her hair matted and her face swollen. She was barefoot and her legs were bruised in numerous places.

"Please," she murmured. "No more." At once both Carl and Gunter perceived she had been raped and beaten.

"We're not here to hurt you," Carl pulled his seat by her cot as she shied away into the corner. "Who are you? Why are you here?"

"I've already told them," she managed. "My name is Violette Szabo. I am the widow of a French soldier, I am here visiting in-laws."

'Szabo,' Gunter repeated softly.

"They've arrested you on suspicion of sedition," Carl said urgently. "They will extradite you to Lyon and hand you over to Klaus Barbie. He's already killed Jean Moulin and he'll kill you. If you help me, I can help you."

"I don't know anything, I've already told them," she insisted. He could see the steely resolve in her eyes and realized the inner strength of the woman despite her fragile veneer.

"Okay," Carl exhaled. "Try this. I am looking for a woman, Angelique Dagineau, from the Dagineau chateau in Montauban. Her father, Francois, came to see me, she's been missing for over a month. I know he's contributed to the FFI here in Limousin. I'm not working for the security forces, I just want to know if Angie is all right."

"I've already told them I don't know anything," she said quietly, "but if I did know anything, I would know that Angelique is okay."

"Gunter?" Carl looked at him.

"If you offered to help me, I can get you out of here," Gunter implored her. "I am a lieutenant with the SD from Berlin. I can have you placed in protective custody. I can assure you that we already have the names of everyone in your network, there is nothing you could tell us that we do not already know. After the war you would be released."

"I've already told them," she stared at the floor, "I know nothing."

Madame Natasha had been dragged and shoved from her damp, urine-stained cell up three flights of stairs to a poorly-lit corridor on the second floor. It was her second day in the bowels of the police station in Lyon where she had been transported from Oradour. Her first night was a traumatic experience in which she was tag-teamed by screaming Gestapo agents for a twenty-four hour period with no food and little water. After only four hours sleep, a chair was hurled against the iron door of her cell before they yanked it open and hauled her away.

At length she was brought to a door where her guards released her and stood at attention. She regained her composure and attempted to smooth her hair as they waited for long minutes. Finally a command was given and the door was opened to permit her entry.

"Madame Natasha, I believe. Please sit."

Natasha swallowed hard, fighting to keep from visibly trembling. The man behind the oaken desk was of average build, yet radiated an aura of absolute authority. His dark eyes probed her features, assessing his captive with the expertise of a man trained in criminal research and analysis, one who knew the streets, who tried men's bodies and souls by fire and knew what made them break.

This man was Klaus Barbie.

"You've traveled a long way, and I know this has been hard on you," Barbie peered into her eyes. "I want to help you, and I know you can be of great help to us. You must understand, and I do want you to understand completely so you can make the right decision. Neither you nor I are soldiers. There is no war between Germany and France, we are united nations under the German Reich. What your accomplices are doing is conspiring to commit treason against your government. I have the authority to release you. All I need is the names of your sponsors and the whereabouts of the stations in your network."

"I'm...I'm just a radio announcer," she looked down at the carpet. "They ask me to read scripts and play music. Everything is tightly guarded, they are all aware of the risks involved."

"I believe this is one of your sponsors," Barbie placed a photo of Gilles Guevremont on the desk before her.

She swallowed hard but said nothing, tears welling in her eyes.

"This man is a high-ranking member of the FTP, a Communist terror group. We understand that he has a personal relationship with you. Is this true?"

"We... we have met socially on a few occasions. I know nothing of his personal life."

"Anything you tell us will be highly useful. What kind of transportation does he have? What places does he bring you to? What does he discuss? What is his usual route in coming to meet you? What is his driver like? We want you to think hard and tell us everything you remember."

"He... he always arrives at the door," she managed. "His driver never speaks, I have never seen his face. He wears a cap, like a chauffeur, pulled over his eyes."

"We have rounded up quite a few people in your network," Barbie exhaled, leaning back in his chair. "Many of them, like you, were facing serious criminal charges, and they made deals to avoid prosecution. More than one of them indicated that you have slept with Guevremont. You are a very attractive woman, you can't tell me that you've had intimate relations with a man you nothing about. Again, you have to realize the situation we're in, and how we can help each other. I am under extreme pressure due to the security threat posed by these gangsters. I don't have the convenience of giving you time to make a decision."

He nodded to his associates by the far wall. There was a tall, bulky man and a small thin man, both dressed in black, standing near a hot plate upon which there were some long metal needles. The odor of burning metal was faint in the air.

"Are you familiar with acupuncture?" Barbie asked nonchalantly. "It is an Asiatic form of therapy in which needles are used at various pressure points to relieve pain. Of course, in the hands of unlicensed practitioners like those fellows, the results can be quite the opposite."

"I can't tell you what I don't know!" she wailed as the men in black came up behind her.

"You will, my dear," Barbie muttered as he stood up and walked out of the office. "You will."

"Carl," Gunter took off his glasses, polishing them in avoiding Carl's gaze. "I've got photos."

"All right," Carl exhaled tautly. "Let me see."

Gunter had called Lyon repeatedly at Carl's request once the word was out that Madame Natasha had been captured. Carl was stricken with horror at the notion that the reason he was unable to find Angie was because she might have been the mysterious Natasha.

Gunter dumped the photos from the large manila envelope and spread them across the edge of the desk where Carl stood. Carl winced as he studied the high-quality images. The woman's face was badly beaten, her hair matted with sweat and blood. The rope used to hang her had cut into her flesh and was just a short time from decapitating her. From her bosom dangled two pulps of burned and scarred fatty tissue. Her arms and shoulders were deeply scarred and burned, and chunks of flesh had been torn from her torso.

"It's not her," Carl grunted.

"Thank God," Gunter was quick to remove the photos from the desk.

"What are we doing here, Gunter?" Carl stalked over to the window, staring into the night. "They kill Helmut, we murder six hundred people. They blow up a railway, we torture and kill female combatants. We were supposed to be bringing German civilization to the world, fighting Communism, restoring law and order to degenerate societies. We've lost our way, Gunter. Do we have to lower ourselves, our standards, to defeat them? Where does that leave us at the end?"

"I wish I had the answers, Carl."

"Keep me posted," he turned to leave. "Somebody somewhere has to know where she is."

"We'll find her, Carl. And you'll be the first to know," Gunter reassured him.

"Carl," Colonel Stadler motioned for him to take a seat in his makeshift office on the grade level of the country house the GMR had provided. "I think we should talk."

"About what?"

"It goes without saying that you're one of my best men," Stadler leaned forward over his desk. "You exceed expectations in almost everything you do out there. You've had a clear vision of our mission and purpose as an SS division, and perform consistently in realizing our goals. My question is this: why have you taken to acting as if you've been reassigned to duty in the Gestapo?"

"I don't follow."

"You've spent more time with Lt. Schweinberg over the last forty-eight hours than you have with your own unit," Stadler retorted. "When you're not with

Schweinberg, I've got you with Heinz Barth, or with your sergeants, driving all over the region into enemy territory without any clearance whatsoever. What I'm at a total loss over is that I've heard you've been evacuating civilians from our theatre of operations."

"Were you good with what happened at Oradour?"

"That's not the point!" Stadler snapped. "Your responsibility to your men, your platoon, this regiment, to me, is first and foremost! You've been running around like some crusader for human rights evacuating women and children from targeted areas of insurgency. How do you know that you haven't helped any terrorists escape? Do you realize how many women we've captured in commission of acts of terror against the Reich? We've taken down Violette Szabo, Madame Natasha, and dozens more in this sweep. God knows how many you've delivered to safety."

"Terrorists don't end up in cages with their children hiding behind their skirts," Carl retorted.

"Your duty is as a soldier, not a human rights activist!"

"That's right, Colonel, I'm a soldier. I never signed on as an assassin."

"There's a difference between defending your country and murder, Carl, don't talk nonsense."

"Then we have to do all we can in drawing and defending that line," Carl insisted. "How many registered kills do you have me at?"

"Two hundred fifty."

"That's what I got. If we do not distinguish between murder and killing enemy, then, when this is over, I go back to the woman I love with the blood of two hundred fifty people on my hands."

"This is what the terrorists have brought to the table!" Stadler argued. "Everything they do is a clear violation of Article I of the Hague Convention! They have no chain of command within a military organization, they wear no distinguishing uniforms, they carry no weapons in plain view, nor do they honor the rules of war. Don't you think your superiors—our superiors—have gone over this? They force us to fight on their level to defend ourselves. Did you know that terror activity has dropped to zero after Oradour?"

"So you're condoning it."

"No, I'm not condoning it! I'm your commanding officer, watch your words!" Stadler grew heated. "See, this is what it all comes down to. This is the SS, you took an oath of loyalty to the Fuehrer. Your superior officers represent his authority. It's the chain of command, it's the tie that binds. You never question orders, if your superior gave you a wrong order then he assumes full responsibility."

"Then who gave the order at Oradour?"

"I sent Adolf Diekmann in there with orders to settle the terror issue," Stadler's tone grew icy. "Reports indicate that he may have acted excessively in doing so. This is really none of your business, Carl, but to clarify your understanding of our situation, the General has gotten numerous queries from Berlin on this matter. A full investigation is pending. The bottom line is, the terrorist network has been crushed and I don't want to hear any more about your escapades behind enemy lines until I give the order!"

"One more thing," Carl countered. "One of my men was involved, Sgt. Von Hoffman. I have reason to believe he was assigned to Barth's platoon without the knowledge or him or Captain Kahn. I intend to find out who gave the order."

"Let me know what you come up with," Stadler said in dismissal.

"Gladly," Carl took his leave.

Major Diekmann stood before Colonel Stadler's desk the next morning, and he was unsettled to see that his superior was beside himself with anger.

"Adolf," Stadler thundered, "this is a serious fuckup. Do you realize what you've done?"

"Sir, I've spent the whole night going over the situation with Major Weidinger," Diekmann said hoarsely. Stadler could see that Diekmann had barely slept and was in a state of near-distraction.

"We are on solid legal grounds, entirely justified in our reactions to the terrorist actions throughout the region."

"Six hundred forty two people, Adolf! Out of these, only two hundred men! You murdered over four hundred women and children!"

"I cannot permit you to refer to this counter-terrorist operation as murder, Colonel!" Diekmann was indignant. "You, of all people, know that we have lost over a hundred soldiers here in France to these terrorists. More than half of these men were tortured to death, look what we found in Tulle alone! And when I think of what they did to Helmut..."

"We are professional soldiers, Adolf," Stadler stared back intently. "When you start taking what happens on the field personally, you lose perspective, you lose control. This is a game of life and death, there is no margin for error."

"I read the Gestapo reports that were compiled by Lt. Schweinberg," Diekmann replied. "He spent a considerable amount of time discussing the incident with Schweinberg. Did you know that there were as many as two and three sewing machines found in the debris of the burned-out houses? There could be no reason other than they were making uniforms for the French Army. Did you know how many vehicles were discovered in the garages? How do you think the village burned so fiercely? It was the explosions of all the gas tanks, not to mention the arsenal in the church that obliterated it so completely!"

"It doesn't make a damned bit of difference whether there were terrorists in the village," Stadler was emphatic. "You gave Captain Kahn full authority to wreak havoc in that village despite the fact there was a weekend crowd from all over the countryside coming to spend time on the lake and shop at the market. There were children from over a half dozen nearby villages there for their monthly physical. Otto turns it over to Heinz Barth, who works alongside Carl Hansen, for God's sakes. Those two spent the entire winter cutting the heads off Mongols in Russia. At least if Carl had gone, there might have been a cooler head prevailing, but who do you end up with? Eric Von Hoffman! What did you think that madman was going to do out there!"

"Sir, my men secured the area before Von Hoffman began the clean-up operation," Diekmann dared not mention the letter from ODESSA. "Everything was under complete control when Heinz's men cleared the area. He left just two squads—twenty-four men - behind to help Eric finish up. We had barely gotten back to the command post before Eric radioed in to report that the male detainees had tried to overpower his Einsatzgruppen guards, and many were shot trying to escape. After that, everything went haywire. Eric sent back a note he found nailed to a door, and I went down to Compain's Bakery and found Helmut's body in an oven, that is in my report. When I returned, I was fully convinced that the terrorists were in the village and gave Barth direct orders to bring closure to the issue. The Mayor was there when I did so."

"Why was the Mayor in your command post?"

"The Mayor approached me when we first came to town. He offered to act as a hostage along with his family, and even suggested that we select thirty persons in exchange for the villagers' release. I dismissed it as nonsense and asked to use his telephone at the Town Hall when I called you to confirm our arrival. After that he was following me around, and I found him useful as a reference guide."

"The Mayor," Stadler frowned, "gave a statement that Barth had promised bloodshed."

"Come on, Colonel!" Diekmann was exasperated. "You've been out there, you know what it's like! They murdered Helmut in cold blood, everyone was hot! Next thing we know, Eric reported that some of the shops were booby-trapped and they were setting off secondary explosions in the Desourteaux Garage. Before we knew it, there were plumes of smoke over the town and the entire strip was up in flames. When Eric got back to the church, apparently some flaming debris was blown by the wind or tossed in an explosion, causing the hidden arsenal in the steeple to detonate. The heat was so intense that it actually melted the church bell in the tower. There was no chance to save anyone."

"Why were the women and children locked in the church, Adolf?"

"For their protection!" Diekmann retorted. "We knew it was the safest place to be, even a terrorist would not think of attacking a church. We never had the slightest clue that the village was booby-trapped. There was not one incident until the menfolk attacked Eric's detail. We sent the town crier out to drum up the civilians and direct them to the square. There were no problems whatsoever, they acted as if it were an air raid drill. We wanted the women and children out of the way so we could secure the area and confirm that the town was free of terrorists."

"So you delegated your authority to Kahn, and he, in turn, to Barth. Now, all of a sudden, we have Von Hoffman, from a different company, and a squad of Einsatzgruppen soldiers from a completely different unit, running the operation," Stadler mused.

"The Einsatzgruppen were mostly Alsatian conscripts, French is their native language," Diekmann was brusque. "It made perfect sense having them there."

"Even though their specialty in Russia was evacuation and special treatment."

"You told us the terrorists had to be stopped at all costs!"

"I cannot deny that I told you the terrorists had to be stopped at all costs," Stadler concluded. "Yet, from any reasonable and logical standpoint, I don't think anyone would disagree that the methods used to carry out the counter-terrorist action at Oradour were not only excessive, but unscrupulous and un-professional. I regret to inform you that you have been ordered to appear before a military tribunal in Berlin upon our return from Normandy, and that you will be relieved of duty within this Regiment pending the outcome of the proceedings."

"I understand," Diekmann lowered his eyes. "I accept full responsibility for what has transpired."

"I was the one who recommended you for promotion to Major," Stadler looked at him ruefully. "I hate like hell to see this happen. I wish you the best of luck."

"Yes, sir," Diekmann gave him the Nazi salute.

The old comrades stared into each others' eyes for a long moment before nodding in mutual understanding as Diekmann took his leave.

One way or another, Diekmann was never to return.

Chapter Eight

Days after the photos of Natasha's mutilated corpse were taken in the town square of a Lyon suburb, they had been distributed to countries across the globe as continuing evidence of Nazi atrocities.

Natasha was barely alive when she was brought to a makeshift gallows and hanged as a traitor in broad daylight. The horrified populace was kept at bay by gunpoint, and Vichy officials soon began circulating the story that she had been tortured by the FTP and was turned over to Lyon for execution. It did nothing to quench the public outrage over the gruesome murder.

The world press had been conducting a media crusade against the Nazis ever since the passing of the Nuremberg Laws legalizing racism in Germany, and continued to document reports of forced evacuation of minorities from the Reich into Eastern Europe. Evidence of concentration camps abounded throughout the Greater German Reich, and proof of genocide was compiled thereafter. The Allies issued a statement that those responsible for the atrocities would be tried as war criminals before a court of international law.

"These bastards," Commander Staunton fumed, posting the photos on a wall along with those taken at Tulle and Oradour. He was meeting with Blackburn and Geronimo at a motel outside of Paris heavily guarded by FFI insurgents. "We've gotten word that the Allied War Command is preparing to declare the SS a criminal organization That means that every single one of those bastards will be liable for charges once this thing's over."

"It's a hard call, Commander," Geronimo lit a cheroot. "I know where you're coming from, but we've got lots of reports about SS troops evacuating civilians out of small towns in the Limousin area to keep them out of harm's way."

"I've heard that rubbish," Staunton retorted. "Supposedly that Carl Hansen fellow led a group that directed some villagers into the countryside while the massacre at Oradour took place. My question is: why wasn't he in Oradour stopping the massacre?"

"He's SS, Commander," Blackburn poured himself a drink. "When in boot camp, members of elite units as he's in would be given a shovel on the training field and ten minutes before their position was overrun by a Panzer tank. They live in a different world than the rest of us. I think Hansen and his friends may have put themselves at great risk by warning those villagers."

"Keep in mind that he's the same vermin who executed a dozen of our operatives outside of Tulle a few nights ago," Staunton reminded him.

"That must've been quite a feat in itself."

"I say, Blackburn," Staunton stared at him, "you sound as if you're beginning to admire that scum."

"Not at all, Commander," Blackburn swirled his drink reflectively before taking a sip. "Not at all."

* * *

"Eric," Carl walked into his room after hearing him arrive at the hotel that evening. "Where have you been?"

"I've been to London to visit the Queen," Eric sniggered, leaning back in his seat by the small desk in the corner of the room. "Ever find your pet frog?"

Carl strode across the room and threw a crushing right cross that sent Eric sprawling across the floor. Eric rolled to his feet but Carl was on him like a cat, grabbing him by his shirt front and throwing a left hook that dropped Eric to the carpet. Eric rolled again, drawing his Luger and pointing it at Carl's face though Carl had already pulled his own Mauser, aiming it between Eric's eyes.

"Is this what they call a Mexican standoff in those American Wild West books?" Eric managed a grin.

"I want to know what you did in Oradour, and by whose authority," Carl demanded. At once the door slammed open, with Michael, Hans and Peter spilling through the threshold.

"Hey, go easy, fellows," Hans interceded quietly. "We don't need this. We've got a big fight ahead and we need every man we can get, especially you two. Let's just take it easy and put down the weapons."

"I told you before I wasn't going to let you be the one to take me out, Carl," Eric gripped the pistol in both hands.

"Well, then, you'd better pull the trigger, because you're not leaving here without telling me what I want to know!"

"Carl! Eric!" Michael insisted. "They can hang you for this!"

"I got no problem with telling you," Eric chuckled, "because there's not a damn thing you'll be able to do about it anyway."

"Try me," Carl scowled back.

"Okay, just give us the guns, and we'll be out of your way," Peter crept slowly between them. Hans and Michael stepped alongside the two and gently grabbed hold of their pistol barrels, pointing them downward before easing them from each opponent's grips.

"Better hope I don't have a hideout," Eric rolled up onto an armchair.

"I'll make you eat it," Carl stared.

"Gentlemen," Peter held up his hands as Hans and Michael led the way out the door, "have at it."

"So," Eric folded his hands in his lap, "where would you like to start?"

"From the beginning," Carl retorted.

* * *

"Is she dead?"

"I told you she wasn't."

"Then put her on the phone!" Jacques Tremblay yelled amidst a stream of sulfurous Corsican expletives and blasphemous oaths.

"This is Sgt. Blackburn," a familiar voice came on the line with a poor French accent.

"I told your flunkies I want to speak to Dominique," he snapped. "She's the one I set this deal up with. My partners and I made a deal to exchange the shipment in exchange for certain arrangements. Do you think I'm going to turn over two million francs' worth of product over to some swamp frogs and find out after the fact that no one's going to honor their end of the bargain? Get your head out of your ass, Blackburn."

"Look, they've been trying to explain the situation to you," Blackburn was patient. "Pierre Bony and Henri Lafont are Gestapo informants. They've been working for the Gestapo since the Nazi occupation."

"What!"

"Why do you think the Bony-Lafont Gang is the only Mob family in Paris able to operate, besides the Corsicans? They've given up all their competitors, and now they're focusing on political targets, enemies of the Reich. The minute you put a bullet in Germaine Gagnon's head you put yourself on a Gestapo list."

"Well, they haven't done too good a job, have they?" Jacques was cocky.

"Think not? Let's try this. Bony and Lafont recruit directly from jails and prisons. Every man they turn out automatically becomes a Gestapo informant by default. Can you imagine how many of them were sent into southern France? The *maquis* is literally crawling with rats, and that's how they infiltrated the FTP and got to the Radio Utopia network. Once they arrested Natasha, we realized we couldn't take a chance by keeping Dominique on the air. As a result, when we began broadcasting reruns of her shows on Radio Free Europe, everyone assumed Natasha and Dominique were one and the same, and the woman was dead."

"So you're guaranteeing political asylum for us with positions in the new Republican government," Jacques insisted.

"That's the deal you made with Natasha, and it will be honored by the French government, you've got my word on that."

"So who am I going to meet? Where are you going to take possession?"

"I want you to call back in forty-eight hours, or we will contact you through Monsieur Le Blanc before them. We have to arrange security and make sure the rendezvous isn't compromised."

"You got a deal," Jacques hung up.

* * *

"Colonel, I believe you're blaming the wrong man for the Oradour incident," Carl revealed.

"Well, Carl," Stadler shook his head dourly, "it seems there are a number of high-ranking Wehrmacht officers who are howling for Diekmann's blood as we speak. General Rommel has personally contacted the Fuehrer and is demanding a court-martial. For your clarification, I had a long discussion with Diekmann earlier, and he accepted full responsibility for his actions, he acknowledges the fact that there was nothing in my tenor that suggested or implied the kind of retaliation that his battalion carried out."

"It was Ruess," Carl insisted. "He set Von Hoffman up to carry out the entire operation. The ODESSA contracted Ruess to investigate a rumor of hijacked SS gold in the Limousin region. Ruess coached Eric to loot the village and burn it down to destroy the evidence, then kill everyone and leave no witnesses."

"SS gold," Stadler looked at him in exasperation. "You want me to implicate Ruess on a charge of mass murder using an urban legend as a motive."

"Be that as it may," Carl was emphatic. "They loaded thirteen vehicles with jewelry, artwork, silverware, furs, precious metals, anything of value they could get their hands on. Did Heinz report bringing anything like that in?"

"Of course not," Stadler stared at him. "I would've been notified immediately if anything like that had been recovered."

Stadler got on the phone and instructed his adjutant to contact OKW in Berlin for feedback on any communications from the Limousin region involving Robert Ruess or the Einsatzgruppen detachment.

"Negative, sir," the adjutant called back within fifteen minutes.

"I want a telegram feed, a radio feed and a teletype set up immediately, tell them I am acting under full authority of General Lammerding in conducting the Oradour investigation," Stadler demanded. "I want all our SS, SD, Gestapo, GMR, Milice[1] and the Vichy police on this. I want everything we have on all communications to and from Ruess and his unit."

Both men sat expectantly as the communication equipment was brought into Stadler's makeshift war room at his chalet. Within minutes the machines were up and running, but the communications officers' efforts were yielding poor results.

"SD intelligence has been restricted by General Kaltenbrunner pending an internal investigation, access denied," the chief officer reported at length. "Gestapo HQ in Berlin is also conducting a top-level inquiry, access denied. Waffen-SS intelligence is in process of compiling its files on the incident, access denied."

"The bastards are censuring the records! It's a cover-up!" Stadler was astonished. "See what you can get on Diekmann and Barth!"

Within minutes the machines began chattering as rolls of paper began spewing intelligence reports onto the carpets.

---

1. French militia

"Make Eric an offer," Carl proposed. "If you can have him transferred and his record expunged, you can turn him as a witness against Ruess. This war's turned him into a psychopath. If you offer him a fresh start he can be rehabilitated. He's doing what he does because he has no hope for a future. This would be his best chance, he has no love for Ruess, he'd give you everything."

"I'm bringing Ruess in," Stadler decided. "He's holed up in his chalet with those Einsatzgruppen troops, he may not go down without a fight. If we go after him he'll think his connections have failed, he's not going to come in to face a charge of six hundred murders. If he does, however, he may think we have an air-tight case, especially if he thinks we turned Eric."

"I think you owe it to Diekmann," Carl agreed.

* * *

"Captain Ruess! The building is surrounded! Come out with your hands up!"

The military police had been reinforced by units of the SD, the Gestapo and the GMR as they cordoned off the area with vehicles, deploying officers along the bushes on all sides of the house. Carl and Gunter rode with the local Gestapo chief and stood with him alongside the patrol car parked parallel to the front of the chalet. Men with submachine guns and pistols positioned themselves around the chalet in various positions of cover, as squad leaders barked instructions over speakers and bullhorns at different points of egress.

"I can get inside a lot quicker than he'll come out at this rate," Carl mused.

"No way, Carl!" Gunter insisted. "This is a police action! We can't afford to lose you. This fellow's history, we can wait him out."

The Gestapo agents rushed the doors on each side with German shepherd attack dogs. The dogs howled and barked but gave no indication that their quarry was near the doors. They next fired gas grenades through windows on each side of the house and got no response.

"He's not home," Carl growled. "Unless he's gone totally berserk, he wouldn't plan on going out like this."

"In view of the circumstances, I think we'd have to deny him the benefit of the doubt," Gunter replied.

At length the GMR officers approached the door with lightweight battering rams. They joined forces in manning the weapon, driving it into the door as they rushed forth in unison. Upon impact, there was a blinding explosion as a booby trap was detonated by the collision. The bodies of the officers and those of the dogs were hurled violently backward in a shower of blood and smoking debris.

"He's not there," Carl walked away from the patrol car in disgust. "I doubt he's even still in France."

"I can put out an all-points bulletin," Gunter insisted. "Do you think he went back to Germany?"

"He's ODESSA," Carl waved a hand as he walked off. "He's probably on a cruise ship on the way to South America."

"Lucky him," Gunter watched the medics moving in to take the bodies away.

* * *

Operation Overlord, the Allies' heavily-planned invasion of Normandy, seemed to be going through without a hitch. An intricate web of deception and misdirection had been woven around the project, leading the Nazis to believe the main expeditionary force would be led by General Patton at Pas de Calais due south. As a result, the dispersed and poorly-coordinated German defensive positions proved vulnerable at numerous targeted landing zones.

One of these, Sword Beach, stretched eight kilometers from Ouistreham to St. Aubin-sur-Mer. It was the furthest east of the landing points, about fifteen kilometers from the strategic town of Caen, a major transportation hub. British General Montgomery's infantry division was met with light resistance as opposed to that faced by the American Army in most sectors, and advanced eight kilometers before being stopped cold by the German defense.

OKW opted to drive a wedge between the forces at Sword Beach and Juno Beach, where the Canadian Army had landed. The German Army's 21st Panzer Division nearly drove to the English Channel in splitting the Allied forces but was forced to withdraw on June 6th. They retreated to a defensive position outside Caen, which Hitler ordered them to hold at all costs. Das Reich Division would be deployed to support the 12th SS Panzer Division Hitlerjugend[2] and the elite Panzer Lehr Division in preventing Montgomery's forces from taking Caen.

Commander Staunton and F Section remained in constant communication with Nancy Wake, who was at the top of the Gestapo's Most Wanted List with

---

2. Hitler Youth

a reward of five million francs on her head. She had coordinated a fighting force of seven thousand men among the *maquis* and was conducting major operations against the Nazis throughout Central France. General Eisenhower, who had made an official statement recognizing the Resistance as part of the French Army, brought an end to the underground movement in declaring the insurgents as legal combatants. This, in turn, resulted in F Section's recall to England for debriefing.

One of their last official acts was to summon the Resistance leaders to a final conference where they would be officially recognized for their efforts. It would be a mini-victory celebration of sorts, allowing them to savor the successes that led to the invasion at Normandy, the impending liberation of Paris and, eventually, France itself.

Blackburn and Sgt. Geronimo walked into the conference room that evening and was greeted by the applause of Resistance leaders who were summoned to the meeting. To the consternation of the small FTP contingent, the turnout was comprised largely of Republicans who had been working to mend their network since the death of Jean Moulin. It was only now that they were able to make their presence known.

The Republican community was galvanized by the murders of Violette Szabo and Madame Natasha, and their efforts in disrupting the Vichy communications and transportation systems were crippling the war effort throughout the South. The meeting was being held on the outskirts of Lyon, where the Vichy forces under Klaus Barbie were being swamped with paperwork on the Szabo and Natasha cases. The SS and Gestapo offices in Berlin, in turn, were inundated by the inquiries on the Oradour case, and as a result, had created a major backlog in the police and military intelligence system. It gave the Resistance forces a short respite during which they saw an opportune time to hold their conference.

Over fifty members of various factions, including the FFI, the FTP, the *Armee Secrete*, the *maquis*, and others who took up arms to liberate France were in attendance. They were treated to the finest French wines available from the Dagineau vineyards, along with a smorgasbord of game meat, chicken, beef, pork, veal, lamb, fish, soups, stews, cheeses, freshly baked bread and pastries. The men munched merrily on the sumptuous offering which followed a prestigious ceremony during which each faction and its members were decorated for their service to France by emissaries of Charles De Gaulle.

The one glaring omission was any mention of Gilles Guevremont throughout the proceedings. The FTP was mentioned in passing and it was announced that a plaque commemorating their efforts would be placed in a memorial institution scheduled to be built in Paris following its emancipation from Nazi rule. Guevremont grew increasingly discomfited as the ceremony wound down, and he and his entourage kept to themselves in a far corner until the conference came to an end. He instructed them to remain on guard outside as he had a final word with the Allied representatives.

"So, gentlemen," Guevremont held his hands out as the other Resistance leaders milled out the door. "I can only assume that your lack of recognition of my contributions towards the war effort was due to the top secret nature of our assignments."

"Sit down, you piece of shit," the three of them turned towards the door as Commander Staunton closed it behind the last of the departing fighters.

"You know," Guevremont shook his head, "I have put up with more than my share of teasing from these two fellows..."

"Sit down," Blackburn said firmly, as Guevremont grudgingly complied.

"Do you know anyone by the name of Jocelyn Perrault?" Staunton paced slowly across the room past Guevremont, who slouched in the overstuffed armchair.

"No," he said softly, enunciating the word emphatically.

"According to our informants in Lyon, the Gestapo and police files indicate that he was arrested near Oradour with a female identified only as Madame Natasha. She would not give up her real name, even unto death, for fear of endangering her friends and family," Staunton said quietly, looking down at Guevremont. "Monsieur Perrault, it seems, was not so chivalrous."

"Madame Natasha," Guevremont raised his eyebrows. "The radio personality."

"One and the same," Staunton continued. "Only the records indicate that Perrault had been picked up and interrogated several hours before he was arrested again with Natasha."

"Interesting," Guevremont nodded.

"Interesting!" Staunton thundered. "You gave her up, you son of a bitch! You made a deal so they let you walk! The Commie bastards in Paris got you off in exchange for Natasha!"

"I don't know where you're getting your information," Guevremont was resentful. "I think it might be in all of our best interests if I took leave of you gentlemen. My men are probably growing restless outside."

"Ah, yes, your men," Blackburn smiled. "I'm afraid they've been detained. I'd daresay they're on their way to Paris as we speak."

"They'll read all about it when they get there," Geronimo unscrewed a cap from a flask of cognac. "I doubt there'll be a place in Paris where you'll be able to hang your hat."

"I'm safe right here in Southern France," Guevremont was smug. "I own Sussac, you know."

"That's part of your problem," Staunton thundered. "We know that you Commie bastards made a deal with the Corsicans right after the Nazi takeover. You agreed to set up a blackmarketing network throughout Southern France, and you all made a mountain of money from it. You didn't lift a finger to help the war effort until we came down here with our bankrolls. Even then, instead of going with the program and fighting the Germans, you started a campaign of kidnapping and murder. You caused the massacres in Tulle and Oradour, and history won't forgive or forget."

"History is written by the victors," Guevremont steepled his fingers. "Paris doesn't belong to the Republicans, it belongs to us. You may hand it over to the De Gaullists, but the people will give it back."

"Maybe you've been away from Paris too long," Blackburn leaned against the wall, lighting a cigarette. "Don't you know the Bony-Lafont Gang and the Commies are in bed together up there? They're making all kinds of sleeping arrangements for after the war, they know their time's almost up. Henri Lafont's got about twenty hit squads down here looking for the morphine smugglers from the Brive job. Don't you think the Reds in Paris might have them take you out while they're at it?"

"So what's your point?" Guevremont exhaled.

"We have a moral obligation to help you out of this in exchange for your services to us," Staunton said ruefully. "Regardless of what we think of you personally, I don't think our superiors would overlook what the FTP was able to do all the time our friends in the FFI had faltered. Therefore, we offer you asylum overseas, out of sight, out of mind."

"My superiors in the OSS have worked out a deal with the Canadian government," Geronimo told him. "You'll get a new identity, a passport, a new start.

We'll arrange for you to take on a mid-level management position at the French Embassy in Montreal."

"It'll be enough for you to comfortably retire on, not to mention the money you and your Alsatian Jewish gangsters made on the blackmarket throughout Southern France," Blackburn said airily. "We know about your Swiss bank account. Of course, we have no idea how many millions you have, but we were able to confirm that you have an account. The Swiss aren't quite as neutral as people think."

"I almost hope you try and raise your flag in Montreal," Staunton sneered as Guevremont rose to leave. "The Quebec Mob'll stick your head on a pike."

"I don't think France will find life after the war to be what it was before," he shot back as he walked out the door.

"Regardless, at least you Commie bastards won't be calling the shots, rest assured of that!" Staunton laughed as Guevremont slammed the door behind him.

* * *

"So this is it," Gunter forced a smile. "Give them hell, eh?"

Carl dropped by the police station in downtown Limoges where the SS clerks under Gunter were packing up their materials in returning to Lyon. Outside, the streets were bustling as the Regiment prepared for its final leg of its trek to Normandy, bartering with local officials for extra supplies as they loaded their trucks for battle.

"I'll give them your regards. Hopefully enough bad guys will be in jail so we won't have any surprises on the way back."

"You know, Carl," Gunter looked at him, "I learned a lot about life, my job, and myself from you, and I will never forget you for that. When I first joined the SS I fully agreed and understood the fact that we would be forced to deal with situations and issues that compromised our morality and ethics as SS officers. I spent a short time in the concentration camp system but requested reassignment to the Einsatzgruppen in order to reevaluate my own significance within the SS. It seemed so cut-and-dried, capturing and executing insurgents, but when we began killing civilians, once again I doubted. When we were redeployed here in France, I thought it would be clearer, more specific, but again it became more confused, more complex. You, however, saw exactly what you had to do, and you did it, without orders, without direction. You took personal responsibility for your actions and acted on your own moral judgment. You saved dozens of lives without once compromising the security of our Fatherland. If only there were more like you, Carl.

What a different legacy we would have left for future generations."

"Follow your own conscience, Gunter," Carl peered into his eyes as they shook hands. "That would make two of us."

"We'll meet again one day, in Germany," Gunter was emphatic.

"If not, pour a drink onto the beach at Normandy when you visit."

"You'll be okay," Gunter encouraged him.

Carl walked out the door to prepare for his date with destiny.

Chapter Nine

It seemed as if a new chapter in the life of Pierre Le Blanc was about to unfold.

He was a gentleman farmer in a long line of landowners in the Limousin region of Southern France. Both his mother and father were Corsicans, and, as such, he had a long family tradition of association with the Union Corse. Although he never personally joined the brotherhood, he had strong connections and was known as a man whose friendship was an important thing. There were many throughout the countryside that came to him for favors, and many of them would risk their lives on his behalf.

After returning home from World War I, he decided to convert a barn on his property into a music hall and restaurant, and added to his fame and fortune with its success. However, after the outbreak of WWII and the Nazi occupation, the informal society of the *maquis* became an underground political entity in which men like Le Blanc occupied a major role. The network was a strategic link between the Republicans, political refugees, the peasants and the government-in-exile, and though the Vichy government did their best to infiltrate its ranks, its code of secrecy was second only to that of the Corsican Mob itself.

Le Blanc was one of those honored at the conference in Lyon, and was assured a position of influence in the new Republic. He was credited for having helped a large number of Alsatian Jews, political fugitives from Paris, and underground activists find refuge along the countryside, particularly in the wheat fields and vineyards growing in abundance along his 1,000-kilometer property line. He was also recognized for his generous contributions to the Resistance and his selfless attempts to intercede on behalf of those persecuted by the Gestapo regardless of personal risk.

Among the riskiest of his efforts was his unusual patronage of the Tremblay Gang. Le Blanc seemed to recognize something of himself in the character of Jacques, something naïve, young and reckless, qualities that he lost along the hard path to maturity. He sent out numerous queries after their initial encounter at the hall, and the more he learned, the more fascinated he was.

Jacques had been partners in a number of projects with Germaine Lafont, and was being groomed for bigger and better things when their falling-out took place. Word on the street was that Germaine had plotted to discredit Jacques during the morphine hijacking in order to eliminate him as competition within his cousin Henri's infrastructure. Jacques had a reputation for being smart, ruthless, fearless, a man of respect. There were many who regretted his expulsion from the gang. It was hoped he would offset the cruelty and treachery of Bony and Lafont as his star continued to rise.

Le Blanc acted as liaison between Jacques and the FFI, and negotiated for the return of the morphine in exchange for substantial compensation by the new Government. He remained self-effacing in order to avoid having Jacques perceive him as a major player, and was successful in harboring the young man in avoiding the numerous police and gangland dragnets seeking to take him down. At last the game had come to its end, and Jacques would soon be delivering the product far beyond the reaches of the Parisians and the Gestapo.

He closed the restaurant early that evening after the few patrons had taken an early leave, glad to be getting home before dark. He was quick to douse the lights after the last cars left, anxious to avoid having newcomers see the lights and rush in before closing. It proved, on this night, to be a grave mistake.

Pierre Le Blanc awoke to find himself in a darkened warehouse surrounded by shadowy figures as he sat chained to a wooden table, seated on a metal chair. He was completely naked and could feel a cool breeze wafting over his skin. His ankles were chained to the chair legs and his arms were stretched across the table, chained by his wrists. His head was pounding from the terrible blow that had rendered him unconscious and he perceived that the sticky feeling over his face was blood.

"So, you're back among the living," a voice spoke crude French. "Thought maybe an old bastard like you wouldn't make it."

"Who are you?" Le Blanc demanded. "What do you want?"

"Who I am is not important," Robert Ruess swaggered out of the shadows, wearing an expensive black silk shirt and suit, his disfigured face in full view. "What I want can be the difference if you live or die."

"I…I know who you are," Le Blanc cleared his throat. "You're Captain Skull-face."

"Can you imagine the nerve?" Ruess grinned at his men, who chuckled like hyenas in the dark. Ruess had contacted ODESSA shortly before vacating his booby-trapped chalet, and they had arranged his passage along with a fresh squad of Alsatian Einsatzgruppen men. Eric Von Hoffman's looting of Oradour had generated over a million francs for ODESSA, but Ruess had further ambitions in mind before leaving the country. As if for emphasis, he dropped a bag containing a mallet and two spikes between Le Blanc's hands.

"You know there will be almost as many people looking for me as there are looking for you," Le Blanc murmured.

"Yeah? Well, that's probably as many people out looking for those Corsican shitbags who knocked off that shipment of morphine in Brive. Nobody knows where they are. Only I think you know where they're going to be."

"They made a deal with the FFI," Le Blanc swallowed hard. "I haven't heard anything of them for weeks."

"You know what?" Ruess signaled two of his men forth to stand on each side of the table. "The Gestapo's had a wire tap on your phone ever since word got out that you were harboring those frogs. It was such a secure line, even my people couldn't plug into it. Then I figured, why waste time trying to cut the line when I could get to the man at the head of the line?"

"I won't give you anything," Le Blanc croaked.

"Want to bet? I tell you, I got hung like a thief on a cross in Russia from these things, and I would've sold my father to the Devil to get loose. I don't think you're going to do any better."

At a signal, the Alsatians pried open Le Blanc's hands and held them palms up on the table as their confederates positioned the spikes, hammering them through into the table. Ruess laughed as Le Blanc's earsplitting screams echoed throughout the warehouse, blood spurting and pooling over the table.

"See, what did I tell you?" Ruess signaled to his other man, who brought forth a car battery and a length of chain. "Now for my next trick. If you don't tell me where the hijackers are meeting with the FFI, we wrap that chain around your balls, hit the battery and watch you try and pull those nails out of the table."

Le Blanc did not respond, and his chair was pulled back so that he screamed out as his hands were torn against the spikes. The Alsatians reached under the table and wrapped the thin chain around his scrotum, then fastened the opposite end to the battery terminals.

"It's hard to say whether you're in a worse situation than I was up on that cross, but I don't think you're going to handle it as well as I did," Ruess grinned.

On signal, one of the Alsatians attached a jumper cable that sent a surge of electricity into Le Blanc's scrotum. The shock effect was enhanced by the perspiration on the metal seat, and as a result, the electrocution was such that the older man's eyes bulged and rolled as foam spewed from his mouth.

"Don't kill him, you idiot!" Ruess kicked at the battery, which the Alsatian quickly disconnected. He grabbed Le Blanc by the hair and signaled one of the men to come forth with smelling salts. Within minutes the glaze in his eyes subsided, and he looked around groggily at his tormentors.

"So what's it going to be? I don't think your plumbing's going to work very well if we do this a few more times," Ruess wiped the blood from Le Blanc's hair onto the clothes strewn around the table. You old guys seem to have trouble in that area in the first place. Why don't you save us all a lot of grief and tell me what I need to know?"

"All right," Le Blanc gurgled. Ruess had the men on either side of Le Blanc step forth with small crowbars, with which they pried the spikes from Le Blanc's hands. He screamed in agony as they did so, and collapsed backwards in his chair. The Alsatians waited until he recovered sufficiently for them to jot down the details of the Tremblay Gang's rendezvous.

"What'll we do with him?" one of the men asked.

"Throw him out on the street," Ruess chortled. "Everyone deserves a second chance."

* * *

The gangsters arrived at the deserted warehouse at 2245 that evening. They drove slowly around the muddy streets surrounding the building, ensuring that no one else had arrived as yet. A gangster exited the lead vehicle and used a bolt cutter to clip the lock from an enclosed parking area. The black vehicles proceeded through the gate, the gangster closing it behind them and wrapping the chain to cover their actions.

The two cars parked by the loading dock where four men emerged from each vehicle. They were eight of the Bony-Lafont Gang's top enforcers, hired by Henri Lafont to settle the matter of

Jacques Tremblay. The dark-suited men trotted up the steps to the loading dock where another man picked the lock in order to gain entry.

"Two million francs' worth of morphine in the hands of that purse snatcher," one of the men snorted as they sought positions around the warehouse floor. "I can't wait to see the look on his face when he realizes what's happening."

"I can't wait to get my hands on that fat little pig Chouinard," another gangster growled as he slipped behind a metal ladder leading to an overhead catwalk. "He's a disgrace to the Parisian Mob. I'm going to have some fun making him squeal before I finish him off."

"Don't forget, we want to try and bring Tremblay in alive," the leader reminded them "He's worth a million francs alive. The other three, dead or alive, either way. It'll be more fun if we can take them in one piece, but if we can't, shoot to kill the others but just take Tremblay down if you can."

The last man to enter the warehouse brought with him a heavy canvas bag carrying sawed-off shotguns that he distributed to his colleagues. They loaded the rifles with the ammo provided, then settled back in the shadows to wait for their quarry.

"Anyone got a light?" one gunman cursed as his lighter failed to ignite.

"You'll be smoking in hell before you meet up with Tremblay," an Alsatian accent called from the rafters.

The Parisians looked up in alarm as a hail of automatic fire began pouring down onto the warehouse floor. Men began screaming and ducking for cover before the lower level erupted with deafening bursts of shotgun fire. Two of the Alsatians were catapulted over the railing above, their entrails splashing on the concrete floor.

"Leave the ransom money on the ground and walk away, we'll spare your worthless lives!" an Alsatian called down.

"What ransom money!" a gangster yelled back. "We were paid to bring the drugs and Tremblay's head back in a sack!"

"Those cutthroat bastards," an Alsatian snarled before he and his men directed their fire at the sound of the gangster's voice. He tumbled from his position in a hail of lead before the return fire caused an Alsatian to collapse in an upper corner.

"Le Blanc lied to the Captain," another man hissed. "He probably misdirected this scum to set this trap. Wait until Skullface finds out, that old bastard will wish we'd fried his balls off instead!"

"Okay, fellows, let's turn up the heat on these Nazi bastards!" a gangster yelled before a rush of flames shot out from beneath a platform. He had come across a stockpile of paint and opened a can, which he spilled across the floor and lit with a match. He sought to lead a charge out the door but was shot dead by the Alsatians from above.

"They can't hit us all, let's make a run for it!" The gang leader barked.

At once there was a flood of light from outside along with the squeal of tires as a fleet of vehicles came sailing down the road towards the warehouse. Both the Alsatians and the Parisians were startled by the sudden arrival and frantically looked about for points of egress from the burning building.

"The building is surrounded!" a voice called from outside. "This is the French Army! Come out with your hands up!"

The roar of laughter resounding throughout the warehouse was as a surreal moment, the anxiety-stricken enemies experiencing a sudden feeling of cama-raderie, knowing they had become as rats in the same trap.

At once one of the gangsters rushed towards a front window and was in-stantly gunned down by the Alsatians.

"You sick Nazi-loving traitors!" the gang leader yelled up at them. "We'll be back on the street in twenty-four hours! They'll hang you bastards from those rafters! Come down and help us fight our way out!"

"We've got time," an Alsatian chortled as the flames began spreading across the warehouse. At once they sent a volley of shots out the front windows, caus-ing a commotion as men cursed and ran for cover. After a short while, a wave of responding fire crashed through the windows and cut down a couple of gang-sters on the warehouse floor.

"Checkmate," the French Army commander smiled admiringly as he took a sip of wine from a small bottle. He stood by his command car in the rear of the cordon surrounding the building

alongside Le Blanc, who relied on crutches for support after the episode with Ruess and his men hours ago.

Le Blanc had been found naked on the street outside the warehouse along the north side of Limoges by one of his gang driving in search of him throughout the town. He recovered sufficiently to call an FFI connection informing him where the Alsatians were being sent to intercept Tremblay. The location was a false one, arranged beforehand in the event Le Blanc

had been captured by the Gestapo, in which event his men were to contact the Parisians with details of the non-existent meeting.

"I'm glad I lived to see this," Le Blanc murmured. "German mercy is a rare thing."

"You really should be in hospital," the commander offered him a cigarette. "They would've killed you, you know. Unless...?"

"Unless they wanted me back on the field," Le Blanc grimaced.

"Get a backup unit to the cathedral," the commander raced out from his vehicle as the sound of gunfire echoed around the warehouse property. "Our agents may be walking into a trap!"

Le Blanc stared bleakly at the flaming warehouse, the sounds of gunfire and screaming men echoing around him. He could only pray that God would allow at least a few righteous men to walk away from the carnage once this terrible night was over.

* * *

Jacques Tremblay led his men into the deserted cathedral just minutes before midnight as scheduled. The gang was unaware that they had escaped the bloodbath at the warehouse and had no knowledge of the triple-cross that had caused it. The Parisian Mob and their FTP connections were scouring the countryside for the morphine but had no clue that the Tremblay Gang had been directed elsewhere.

"There's no one here," Marcel said as they proceeded slowly into the darkened church with their guns drawn. He stopped to dip his fingers into the holy water font and blessed himself, causing the others to break out in laughter. He then stepped between one of the aisles of pews and knelt in a short prayer.

"Cut that out," Lucien insisted. "You'll bring us bad luck."

"I think," Marcel blessed himself at prayer's end, "we can use all the help we can get." At that, Jean-Paul hawked and spat a gob of bloody phlegm onto the floor.

"This is the house of God!" Marcel was wide-eyed.

"That's disgusting," Lucien snapped. "You need to see someone about that."

"Spread out," Jacques ordered. "Jean-Paul, Lucien, you take the upstairs, check out the front and back. Marcel, you guard this door, I'll check the sacristy."

Jacques trotted towards the baptismal font to the right of the altar and carefully wedged the metal briefcase between the basin and one of the kneelers. From there he stealthily made his way towards the sacristy and slipped through the heavy wooden door.

Marcel heard a soft thump near the entrance and froze momentarily before realizing that the wind might have blown an acorn from a nearby tree. Yet he realized that the nearest trees were along the walkways on either side of the cathedral. He they attributed the noise to debris being blown by a strong gust, but on second thought decided to investigate.

His last conscious moment was the bayonet driven into his belly skewering his insides and spilling them onto the church steps. He tried to scream out before losing consciousness but a gloved hand covered his mouth as he was dragged behind the door.

The intruder darted up the stairwell leading to the balcony and came face-to-face with Jean-Paul. He fired a shot from his Mauser and hit Jean-Paul between the eyes, hurling him backwards over the balcony, dropping him to the floor where he landed with a resounding smack. Lucien emptied his Beretta in the direction of the muzzle flash, and the return fire caught him twice in the chest, left of center. Lucien fell backwards into a bench and was dead when he hit the floor.

Jacques emerged from the sacristy from the entrance behind the altar and fired at the balcony, taking refuge behind the long marble structure. The intruder plunged from the balcony and ducked behind the row of pews to Jacques' right so that they were diagonally across from one another.

"Give up the morphine," Robert Ruess called over to him. "Walk out the door and I'll let you live."

"You're a dead man, you Nazi bastard," Jacques yelled back. "They'll take me back to Paris when they get here. They'll cut your balls off for what you did in Oradour."

"They won't make it in time," Ruess jumped to his feet.

Jacques rose from his cover and fired at Ruess, who dove and rolled across the floor as the head of a statue of the Virgin Mary exploded behind him.

"I'll be sending you to hell for that," Ruess scoffed at him.

"Is that where my contact is?" Jacques ducked behind a pillar, closing in on Ruess' position.

"Your contact went to the wrong address," Ruess scooted behind the rear pew, trying to determine Jacques' position. "Should've been one of my death squads waiting for him. I followed

that old shitbag Le Blanc after his friends picked him off the street. It wasn't hard to find out where you were going to be."

"There are people on their way out here right now!" Jacques warned. "You still have a chance to correct your mistake!"

"The people outside?" Ruess laughed. "I cut their heads off and set their car on fire. You frogs are as clumsy as you are stupid!"

Jacques assessed the situation and made his move. He dove and rolled down the pew, coming to his feet ten meters from the sound of the voice. As he did, Ruess appeared from behind the last pew with his gun trained on his opponent's nose as was Jacques'.

"Drop it," Ruess barked. "Walk out and I let you live."

"Make your move, Nazi scum!" Jacques yelled. "I got you right between the eyes."

"Game over, gentlemen," a voice called from the shadows where Jean-Paul's body lay in a pool of blood. "Robert, stand down, I'll take it from here."

Both men watched in amazement as Carl Hansen stepped into the dim lights of the massive chandelier hanging from the domed ceiling, his sawed-off shotgun trained on Jacques.

"You back down, Lieutenant," Ruess pointed his Mauser at Carl. "I'm on special assignment from Major Wulf to deal with this matter. He never said a word about you. We knew you had your own agenda."

"There're warrants all over the Reich for your arrest, Robert, don't make me laugh!" Carl swung his shotgun towards Ruess. "You're letting Diekmann burn for what you had Eric do in Oradour. You'll answer for that."

Gunter's last Easter egg for Carl was the intercepted calls between Le Blanc and Tremblay in which Le Blanc gave Jacques the alternate meeting place in case of his arrest. The call that Ruess was able to tap into was gimmicked by the SD.

"You know I'm your master at this game, Carl," Ruess alternated his gun barrel between Carl and Jacques. "I taught you all you know, but not all I know."

"Bullshit," Carl taunted him. "We all know why you came out on the field so often, just so you could watch me work."

Keep talking, you Nazi bastards, Jacques calculated the timing he would need to hit both Germans in the face. He knew that, if he failed, they would converge upon him and kill him, there would be no second chance.

"Well, then," Ruess sneered at Carl, "within the half hour you can explain to the Devil in Hell exactly what it is you're doing there."

"You can't take us both, you ugly piece of shit," Jacques finally turned his gun on Ruess. "I know who you are, you're Captain Skullface!"

"You'll both take that name to hell with you," Ruess smirked.

"Give the Devil my regards when you get there. Carl, don't make a mistake here. I'm on a mission to retrieve the product."

"That's funny, it's not what they told me," Carl sneered. He wrenched a grenade from his belt, having it rigged so that the pin pulled as he did so. They watched in awe as he tossed the grenade past Jacques towards the baptismal font in the alcove before diving for cover. The device exploded in seconds, smashing Jacques into a nearby pillar and sending Ruess flying through a stained glass window. Carl waited until the noise subsided, regaining his feet as a cloud of dust and the odor of cordite and medicine filled the air.

"You Frenchmen," Carl walked over and kicked Jacques' gun away as he sat in a daze, propped against a shattered pew. "Always the hard way."

"This is the French Army!" a loudspeaker blared from outside. "The building is surrounded! Come out with your hands up!"

"I'd tell them to be gentle with you, but I really don't think that would be the prime topic of discussion," Carl bade Jacques farewell. "At least you'll have Ruess to keep you company. I'll bet you two have lots in common."

Jacques watched as Carl rushed past him towards the demolished alcove and disappeared into the dust cloud. He tried to reach his gun but the wind had been knocked out of him and he was stunned by the impact of his skull bouncing off the pew against which he lay. He forced himself away from the pew as he heard men yelling orders in French along with the sound of running feet. At length he saw a figure standing over him, a rifle pointed in his face.

"Jacques Tremblay," the rifleman grinned. "Doesn't look like your friends fared out so well."

"Go to hell," he choked.

"I'd love to send you there," the rifleman replied, "but unfortunately the people who make the decisions around here have arranged to have you brought back alive. We were told to tell you

that your deal still stands, you'll be rewarded handsomely once the Nazis are driven out of France."

"Why don't you start with those two bastards outside?" Jacques gurgled.

"Monsieur Alain," another rifleman approached him as he assessed the carnage inside the church. "There is no sign of anyone outside."

"What?" he demanded, whirling towards his comrade. "We have over thirty armed men and four trucks outside, and you tell me that two Nazis slipped away?"

"I have no idea how many there were," the man replied. "There are none now."

The riflemen hauled Jacques to his feet and dragged him screaming and cursing from the cathedral. Their comrades continued to spew curses and sulfurous oaths as they searched the perimeter with a fine-toothed comb, but the commandos were nowhere to be found.

Chapter Ten

Francois Dagineau plodded down the carpeted steps of the two-story chalet, somewhat nettled that someone would be coming to his door at so late an hour. Most of the politicals had the good sense to call beforehand, as did all of his neighbors in Montauban. He would have heard the crunch of gravel if someone had driven to the front porch, which indicated that someone had either walked or had been dropped off at the gate. The light patter of rain against the windows apparently did not stop his visitor from venturing this far into the countryside at such an hour, well past nine PM.

He opened the door and stood astonished at the sight of the tired young woman, her beautiful features dampened by the rain, strands of her hair curling around her cheeks. She wore a dark hat and coat from which the rain rolled in drops onto the marble steps.

"*Angie!*"

"Hello, Papa."

He reached out and crushed her in his arms as if she had returned from the dead. His eyes filled with tears, and he could not find words, nor speak them if he did. It was all he could do to keep from sobbing as she held him close, hugging his neck.

"My child," he finally released her, holding her arm as if afraid to let her go were she to disappear again. "My daughter. Come, come to the fire, oh my Angelique."

He released her long enough to allow her to remove her hat and coat, then hung it up for her before taking her around the waist and taking her to the couch. They sat in each others' arms, gazing at the fireplace for a long time without speaking.

"I could not lose Carl to those madmen, Papa," she finally managed, tears streaming down her cheeks. "When he first came back to me he was so proud, oh, so proud of that uniform. You know how idealistic he is, what a pure heart he has. I couldn't bear to think that they would deceive him as they deceived the entire German nation. It was beyond fighting for my country, I was fighting an evil empire for the soul of the man that I love."

"Why couldn't you have told me, Angie? You broke my heart," he touched her cheek, weeping quietly.

"I know how much you love me, Papa, and I know that you would have never let me go, or that you would have had me followed and your people would have interfered with what I had to do," she insisted, holding his hand tightly. "All the time I was gone I thought of you. My greatest fear was of getting caught, and not because of what they would have done to me, but what it would have done to you."

"Oh, my Angelique," he hugged her head so that he could hold it against his breast, "my God, my God would have never done that to us, praise His Name."

"I think it's almost over," she said quietly. "The Americans and the British have landed, Frenchmen are taking up arms all over the country under command of De Gaulle. The Nazis are retreating, the traitors in the Vichy government are turning their coats again. It is a matter of time before the Germans sue for peace."

"What were you doing, my precious?" he cupped her chin so he could look into her eyes. Without her makeup she had an angelic beauty that matched the name they had given her at first sight.

"I can't tell just yet, Papa," she touched his hand. "Soon, very soon, but not yet. I only ask you one thing, in the name of Mama, I pray to you."

"Anything, my darling," he said intently.

"I ask you do all in your power to protect Carl when he returns," she beseeched him. "I know he is with the SS, and they will be hunting him, but I would die if something were to happen to him."

"Everything and anything I can, my child, I swear it."

"Oh, Papa, thank you, thank you!" she threw herself into his Arms. They sat weeping in exultation for a long, long while.

The orange, hazy skies shone with a sickly pale light as smoke and flames greedily consumed the atmosphere. The incessant chatter of gunfire echoed beneath the roaring explosions that shook the earth. Dying men screamed in agony as the living raced madly across the surreal landscape, praying only to survive. The soldiers were dwarfed by the war machines facing each other across the seashore, crowding each other in adding to the maelstrom.

It was June 28th when elements of the 2nd Panzer Division of Das Reich under General Lammerding finally arrived at the town on Noyers-Bocage, just south of the strategic transportation hub of Caen. Major Wulf's Recon Unit, 'First To Arrive, Last to Leave' as always, roared onto their scene on the motor-bikes and managed to dislodge a British platoon positioned along the outskirts of town to halt their advance.

"Okay, men," Captain Kahn called his lieutenants together. "Here's the plan. Carl moves left, Heinz moves right, we take out any defensive units along the way, clearing the road for our motorized battalions bringing up the rear. Instruct your sergeants to move their squads by standard procedure, fire and cover, watch your flanks, don't get split up. If there's a heavy concentration of enemy, wait for tank backup, do *not* go for the Iron Cross, there'll be plenty for time for that on the beach. We're looking to run our Tigers straight up the middle once the enemy comes out to meet us, we'll split their ranks and break their jaws. May God be with you, Heil Hitler!"

"If I don't see you on the beach, I'll meet you in hell," Carl grinned wolfishly as the two lieutenants grabbed one another and pounded each other on the back.

"We'll be rejected by the Devil, you know. God will have no choice but to take us in," Heinz Barth smiled softly as he walked off to rejoin his platoon.

"Okay, guys," Carl turned to Eric, Hans, Peter and Michael. "According to the brassy asses, we'll be hooking up with the 12th SS Panzer Division of the Hitler Youth in reinforcement of the 21st Panzer Division, which is standing by to be overrun by the British 3rd Infantry division and whatever else is coming in behind them. I want to move along parallel streets so that we can converge on either side of a building sheltering enemy. I want Eric and Hans' squads to cover each others' movement along the south sides of the buildings, I'll move with Peter and Michael's squads. Eric, you'll be watching for British units coming from the south to reinforce their units in the city limits. I'm looking for pockets of resistance or possible backup from the Hitler Youth. Okay, let's move it!"

The twelve-man squads moved by fire and cover, leapfrogging street after street, using doorways, wrecked vehicles and street posts as shields as they took turns guarding their teammates' progress. In a short time they had raced through the embattled town, exchanging random shots with British snipers though sustaining no casualties. At length they reached the northernmost edge of town where the 21st Panzer Division were positioned, exchanging intermittent artillery fire with the British 3rd Infantry situated about five kilometers away.

"How's it hanging?" Carl greeted an artillery captain, engrossed in his survey of the forward British positions through his field glasses. "I heard you were standing by to be overrun."

"Maybe someday, but not tonight, Lieutenant," the captain retorted, lowering his glasses to face Carl. "Kingdom Division? Glad you made it. We heard you tore the Russians a new asshole before you came out here for the frog leg buffet."

"Our guys are just down the road, we're recon," Carl replied. "Look, I'm thinking of hitting the beach and see if we can pull some of our guys out of there. If I can help them regroup, maybe we can hold positions for the Hitler Youth to move in and give us some breathing room, maybe shove the Limeys further south."

"Who the fuck do you work for, Lammerding?" the captain squinted at him. "They rename the Division after him and now he thinks he's going to win the war singlehanded? Don't forget, he still answers to Rommel, he'll have to answer if you and your platoon disappear out there."

"We won't, Captain," Carl reasoned, his dark mane billowing in the wind. "Look, it only makes sense. Our air recon has reported a large number of fractured units out there seriously needing backup. We can help them push the Brits back long enough to let Hitler Youth move in."

"Don't get your hopes up over Hitler Youth," the captain returned to his field glasses. "Bunch of punk kids who should still be in boot camp. You secure an area and let Hitler Youth relieve your position, it's a fifty-fifty chance the Brits'll be chasing your asses right back here."

"Watch our backs, I'm calling up my sergeants," Carl decided.

"Have a nice life," the captain continued watching the British front lines.

Carl commandeered a couple of idle trucks and hitched a ride along with his platoon down to the beach. The commandos clambered out of the vehicle and stared bleakly at the carnage along

the shoreline as Carl called his sergeants together.

"Okay, guys, let's hope this isn't the last play of the game," Carl grinned wolfishly. "We'll run the same play, Eric and Hans wide left, Michael and Peter wide right on my lead. We'll surround that rockline up ahead; once we're in position, Eric'll call the next move on the left flank. If it's friendlies, we'll help them regroup and get back on the field, if it's enemy, kill anything that moves. Whatever happens, it's been a blast, fellows!"

"My father once beat me unconscious while we were having a family picnic at the beach," Eric smiled, taking his shirt and boots off as Carl watched quizzically. "He said that people should have more respect for their clothing than to wear their shoes on the beach. It's been one of my rules ever since."

His men, grown used to Eric's eccentricities, dutifully removed their own shoes and shirts. Carl suddenly regretted that he had not taken a closer look at Eric's relationship with his squad, yet realized there had never been any real indication that Eric had been capable of an Oradour, with or without Ruess.

"Go with God, Eric," Carl exhaled resignedly.

"God left this game a long time ago, Lieutenant," Eric smiled softly. "Okay, men, let's get to killing!"

Carl watched them charge barefoot down the left flank for about a quarter kilometer alongside Hans' squad, the two squads splitting as they approached the southern edge of the rockline. As Hans' soldiers veered right, a mortar shell landed squarely in front of Eric's squad. Eric continued his charge down the beach through a great cloud of sand and gunsmoke, his men following blindly as they disappeared from view.

"Let's get them!" Carl bellowed, leading the charge to the northern edge of the rockline. The commandos raced to the right flank, approaching the rockline before Carl signaled them to split ranks. Carl signaled Peter to follow him wide to the right, and they dashed around the towering rocks to confront the enemy on the opposite side.

The SS men turned the corner and ran directly into a platoon of British soldiers, many of them wounded, some armed with rifles, the rest carrying only pistols or bayonets. Carl emptied his Mauser into the crowd before diving directly into their midst, his men following suit. The British were unable to fire at such close range and thus forced to engage in hand-to-hand combat.

Carl pulled out his bayonet and began hacking frenziedly at the enemy, clearing a path for his men to follow. They braced each other, standing back-to-back in staving off their desperate opponents. Yet it seemed as if they would be taken down by the weight of numbers until there was a great crash at their rear flank.

Michael's men had spilled through the rockline and converged upon the enemy, falling upon them with wild-eyed vengeance.

Within minutes the English lay dead or dying on the blood-caked sand, having proved no match for the seasoned SS fighters. Carl dragged one grievously wounded man to a seated position.

"Where's your backup!" he demanded in guttural English, holding the man's lapels with his left hand while grabbing the partially-severed left arm in his right hand. "I'll tear this damned thing off, spare yourself the pain!"

"All right, damn you!" the man screamed from the pressure. "The next troop carrier arrives in five minutes! They'll be charging straight at us!"

"Bad news, Carl," Peter peered over the rocks at the bloodsoaked shoreline. "They're ahead of schedule."

"Disarm these men, carry whatever you can, toss whatever you can't over the rocks, and jump out firing!"

At once there was a rain of weaponry cascading over the rockline to the surprise of the charging platoon of Englishmen, causing them to slow their advance just before the SS men began hurtling over the rocks and firing upon their position. The soldiers were taken aback by the unorthodox tactics of the Germans, who were racing at full speed on either side of them yet hitting their targets with deadly accuracy. The British troops returned fire, cutting a number of SS men down, but suffered great loss and were caught out of position as the SS men charged with fixed bayonets. Once again, the ferocity of the commandos and their superior speed and conditioning resulted in a bloody and decisive SS victory.

Carl left one of his men behind to watch over the wounded as he led the others, nineteen in all, including Michael and Peter, to a large boulder overlooking a crevice along the rocky shoreline. Below them appeared a disheveled crowd of enemy troops which had converged there after failed attempts to reach higher ground beyond the shore. They appeared dazed and confused and were taking stock of their wounded and remaining supplies.

"All right, men!" Carl shouted at the band of survivors. "We can either wait here and get killed or captured, or kick these dogs back into the sea like we said we would! They're almost out of ammo and have as little chance as we do of getting reinforced or resupplied! Let's pick up what we have and fight with everything we've got! We'll finish the game like men, hail Hitler and may God have mercy on our souls!"

They peered over the precipice and saw the horde of disconnected British soldiers making their way along the rockline, possibly as many as one hundred fifty to two hundred men. Among them were the staggered and wounded, yet those fit for combat well outnumbered the Germans. They carried rifles, pistols, bayonets and knives, and Carl determined that, at least, they were as poorly armed as their German foes.

With the bloodcurdling cry of a Valkyrie, Carl hurtled over the rocks and down into the midst of the British invaders. His men saw no alternative other than to follow, dropping as demons as they fought with frenzied desperation in being surrounded by an unprepared enemy. They watched Carl's meter-long machete blade come alive as a flesh-eating serpent, swirling in patterns as it carved open faces and chests, split skulls and severed limbs. The Brits flung themselves in force against the tiger-muscled attacker but pushed themselves into harm's way, struck down in showers of blood before being able to defend themselves against his onslaught.

The Germans did their best to match Carl's manic ferocity, parrying and thrusting though many were struck by pistol and rifle fire or struck by the fatal bayonet thrusts of trained British commandos. They looked desperately to Carl, who was as a bloodspilling whirlwind, releasing showers of gore with every slash, stab and slice. Entrails spilled across the sand as Carl disemboweled his foes with a murderous swipe of his blade. One man wobbled back towards Carl's comrades with his head gone from his shoulders. Another man's legs buckled as his jaw dangled from the torn cheek of his face. Yet another man was in the path of Carl's dive from a rock ledge, and his arm dangled from his shoulder, nearly chopped off at the collarbone.

"Come on, there's an opening, it's glory or the grave!" Carl roared as the Germans could see daylight between the rockline, the British lying dead or dying along the aperture. He led the charge as they followed him in a near-panic, bullets and bombs careening and exploding in a cacophony around them.

Elements of the Canadian 1st Army and the British 2nd Army had converged along the beach, fighting desperately to join the fray which continued to surge back and forth as the Germans and the Allies remained in a death struggle for the path of life to Caen ahead. The Falaise Gap had nearly proven to be a death trap for the 7th Army, the 5th Panzer Army and the Panzer Group Eberbach. Nearly 80,000 German troops were committed to a war of attrition in the area southeast of Caen, and Carl's Company had chosen to sacrifice itself in a vain attempt to disrupt the flanks of the advancing British army group.

From the aerial view of British reconnaissance planes, commanders could only watch in alarm as Carl's generic platoons continued to ebb and surge as a destructive tide against the irresistible flow of British and Canadian troops onto the shore. Carl would lead his men into suicidal charges that broke the jaws of pincer maneuvers, allowing the Germans to regroup and form a wedge into disorganized formations of leaderless sub-units. The British yelled commands into their radios in vain, knowing full well that an artillery barrage or an incendiary strike were impossible under such conditions. Even their tank squadrons rolled uselessly along the perimeters as they were unable to enter the rocklines where Carl and his men staged their massacres.

Eventually Carl and his men watched from a rockline, almost exhausted by their efforts in slaughtering enemy although outnumbered five to one. They watched bleakly as a fresh swarm of British soldiers charged from a rock formation about fifty meters ahead, wild-eyed and frantic in their desperate charge to adapt and overcome to this deadly environ. The Germans looked desperately to Carl, who was caked by the blood of his victims though he also bled from multiple cuts and wounds. His hair was matted by the blood of the dead and his features were unrecognizable, smeared by the bone and gristle of his enemies.

"All right," Carl finally relented. "To engage in another charge like this will be suicide. We'll retreat towards those hills due east and reposition for another assault. Hopefully we'll converge with a friendly unit so they can bear the brunt while we catch our second wind!"

Carl and his men were never allowed that second wind. They had been ordered by the commanders of Panzer Lehr and 12th Hitlerjugend to reinforce the German defensive line eight kilometers south of Bayeux. Sleepless for over three days, exhausted by combat and near-starved and dehydrated, Carl's patchwork battalion were scattered like tenpins by the 7th Armored Division of British Lieutenant General Bucknall's XXX Corps. He was one of the only survivors of the carnage, and troops of the 2nd Company SS Heavy Tank Battalion 101 were astonished by the handful of men returning to their ranks as walking dead.

"It must be hell out there," Lt. Michael Wittman, the legendary hero of the Battalion, came up to Carl and handed him his canteen as the rest of the men slumped to the ground along the staging area overlooking the town of Villers-Bocage. "There's the Devil to pay, and, by God, they will pay!"

"These men deserve the Iron Cross just to breathe after what they've endured," Carl winced, a grievous side wound impairing his own breathing. "Make sure their names are recorded for what they've done."

"We've got to get you to hospital," Wittman insisted as he saw the blood trickling down Carl's pants leg.

"I saw two million francs' worth of morphine blasted into dust in a cathedral in Limoges," Carl grunted painfully. "If we've anything left, share it with these men and those about to give their blood for the Reich."

"What about you?" Wittman asked softly.

"I've got everything I need," Carl managed a smile. "There is an angel waiting for me."

Wittman decided that Carl had seen the death angel, and grudgingly turned his back to return to command of his troops. Carl, in turn, walked down a sloping road and stared fervently into the starry night sky.

He thought of Angie, and how she could most certainly see the same moonlight that he was seeing, just a couple hundred kilometers away. He thought of her smile, her eyes, her lips, her wonderment, everything that was her, and that he would determine to die in her arms, not here.

He thought of Robert Ruess, how he had managed to manipulate his situation, grasp victory from the shadows of death, and endure, survive, even prosper, despite whatever he had become. Ruess was a war criminal, hunted by the SS itself...yet he survived. It was on this premise that Carl decided that he had sacrificed enough.

The war was lost. He would spend whatever he had left in returning to Angie.

He full well knew there was the possibility of Einsatzgruppen units or Gestapo agents lurking along the rear lines, waiting to entrap a wounded soldier seeking refuge from the horror. Carl was certain that he would cleave the skulls of any death squads in his path, yet he saw no point in giving them the advantage of first strike. Furthermore, his insignia as a Waffen-SS soldier would leave no doubt that he had abandoned a Division whose motto was victory or death.

As he crossed the fields of death, he began trading his clothes with dead regular Army soldiers. Legless corpses offered shirts as freely as did armless men pants. Carl began running, foraging through duffel bags for food and water as he sprinted across the battlefield. He found a Mauser and holster that would provide him with sufficient protection. He wasn't sure of where or how, but he would make it back to Angie.

He considered the distance of his journey back to Montauban from whence the trek had begun. Only his motorcycle was part of the flaming wreckage strewn across the fields of Normandy. The sheer irony of the situation stunned Carl. He lurked in the shadows, avoiding people, creeping through forests as the French people breathed the sweet air of freedom. Just weeks before, the Division was treated as diplomatic good-will envoys. Now he was a fugitive who ran the risk of getting lynched by zealots.

Knowing his appearance was a giveaway, Carl stole onto a farm and snatched clothes off a line as the madame left on an errand. It enabled him to travel more openly, improving his travel time. At length he realized he stood a better chance of making it if he saved his strength during the day and continued his trek at night. His biggest task would be in avoiding the groups of revelers riding in trucks, in wagons, on bicycles, spreading the news of Das Reich's disaster. The blood had stained his flannel shirt so that he would easily be seen as a deserter or straggler. A vengeful mob hearing his accent would string him from a tree at best.

At one farm he came across a pail of fresh milk, probably left behind by a farmboy caught up in the revelry. At another he found rags with which to bind his wound. The bleeding had slowed by now, but it burned like fire and it would have to be tended to. His main concern was shelter, and to his utter joy, it came in a deserted hayloft where he was able to drift into dreamless sleep.

Carl was suddenly roused by the snap of a twig close to the bush beneath which he lay, and rolled into action. He saw the combat boots of the intruder, and lunged with a sweeping windmill kick that took the legs from under them. With a mighty lunge he was atop them, holding his bayonet to the trespasser's throat.

"What do you want?" Carl demanded in French.

"Don't kill me, I can't understand you!" the boy cried in German before Carl released him.

"Who are you?"

"I am Henrik Kersten from Bitburg!" the boy managed as Carl helped him to his feet. "I am with the 1st Squad, 3rd Platoon of the 2nd Regiment of 12th Hitler Youth. We were separated from our unit at Bayeux and nearly overrun.

The Canadians chased us for many kilometers but we managed to escape. We've been wandering east trying to make contact with friendly units but we're lost."

"Where are the others? How old are you, anyway?"

"Fifteen," the boy replied. At once a group of six boys and one girl ventured forth from the treeline protecting the bushes where Carl found rest. They all carried bayonets and wore fatigues but had no rucksacks.

"Unbelievable," Carl shook his head.

"That is a terrible wound," the girl winced. "If you have anything to work with I can reset it, I'm a nurse."

"If you touched it you'd be a dead nurse," Carl grimaced. "Do you have anything to eat?"

"We haven't eaten in almost two days," Henrik replied. "We've managed to forage crops along the way but it's hard, the farmers are watching for thieves."

"Well, I'll be damned if I'll starve to death on account of farmers," Carl growled. "All right, follow me, stay in line, two meters between each of you, watch my hand signals, no talking!"

They force-marched about twenty kilometers before coming into sight of a farmhouse and barn amidst a wheatfield cordoned by a single strand of barbed wire supported by a long line of fenceposts. Carl surmised that it was merely to delineate the property rather than keep livestock within.

"Which of you can milk a cow?" he asked them. The girl, Ingrid, raised her hand.

"Good," he continued. "The bunch of you will move in, two deploying to either side to cover the flanks. When the rest of you get to the barn, two of you will guard either side while Ingrid milks the cow. Henrik will bring the pail back here. Milk will tide us over until we cross the border, which should take another day."

The teens were about to cross the wire when the click of a rifle trigger stopped them cold. Carl cursed himself a fool for not having been aware, realizing that his concern for the children had dimmed his senses. He started for his bayonet but realized that he might be exposing them to danger, weaponless as they were.

"Who are you? What are you doing here?"

"I'm a volunteer with the FFI," Carl replied in French. "My unit was shattered by retreating German forces along the outskirts of Bayeux. We prepared a killing field about thirty kilometers southwest of the battle but their armor allowed them to scatter us. I came across these children; they were conscripted by the German Army but became detached from their units. All they want to do is go home. Have pity, Monsieur."

"My wife and I are Christians," he replied. "I've been forced to patrol the field due to all the banditry in the area. The criminals in the FTP are having their day with the collapse of the Vichy government; they're stealing and robbing throughout the countryside. All of our chickens have been stolen and our vegetable patches picked clean. Still, my wife would not forgive me were I to let these children go hungry. Come, friend, bring them to the house."

Carl and the man, Monsieur Lemieux, led the children to the house where his wife was taken aback by the bedraggled children in their dirty uniforms. They were directed towards the barn where they could wash and change into spare overalls stored there over the years. When they returned, their eyes widened as saucers at the sight of fresh pitchers of milk and loaves of bread on the table, and cabbage stew on the stove.

The teens munched happily as they communicated through Carl, acting as interpreters between the Lemieuxes and the teens. He was slightly disgruntled at first but eventually learned that the kids had attended the same high school and were recruited by Hitler Youth against their parents' wishes. They were poorly trained, little more than scouts when they were given rifles and placed on the field. They were intended strictly as reserve backup but were forced to fight as the Hitler Youth was decimated by the relentless Allied onslaught.

"Let me change your dressing, sir," Madame Lemieux entreated him. Carl grudgingly relented, and she took him into the bedroom. She winced at the severity of the gash, nearly a centimeter deep and almost a quarter meter long. She filed it with antiseptic and balm before padding it with gauze and taping it heavily.

"You should be in hospital," Monsieur Lemieux insisted. "I'll take you at once."

"I promised these children I'll take them home," Carl declined. "God bless you for what you've done. We'll be leaving once they've finished supper."

"You're not a Frenchman," Lemieux nodded towards the tattoos near Carl's heart, a small one identifying his blood type and the larger one displaying the wolf's hook symbol of the Kingdom.

"Don't think me a liar," Carl replied. "I was trying to protect the children."

The Lemieuxes joined hands with him and they prayed for a time before rejoining the children, who were finishing the last of a sumptuous meal. After a short time, they graciously thanked the couple before resuming their journey. They were told to keep the overalls, which helped disguise them further though they were forced to keep their uniform blouses on. Carl saw these as dead giveaways, continuing to lead them through the treelines whenever possible. As darkness fell, Carl permitted them to march in closer rank though insisting on noise discipline at all times.

He discerned movement along the road and signaled them to caution as they crept through the bushes along the roadside. He was about to lead them further into the trees when a floodlight stopped them in their tracks.

"Stop where you are!" a voice bellowed. "Come out with your hands up!"

Carl led the teens forth, and he cursed and swore at the sight of a squad of *Milice* being led by four trenchcoated Gestapo agents.

"So!" the Gestapo leader swaggered forth. "Nine of you, wandering around in uniform blouses after dark. Why would I not think you've deserted your units?"

"They're Hitler Youth, I brought them on a field trip from Bitburg," Carl retorted. "We got waylaid by the Communists outside of town. Farmers were kind enough to donate the clothing. Most of the damned frogs out here wouldn't give us the time of day. Why do you think we're walking?"

"It'll be a simple matter to take your fingerprints and forward them to Berlin," the leader sneered. "If they come back as military, we'll hang you all as deserters."

The trembling children were surrounded by the rifle-bearing *Milice*, the Gestapo agents carrying submachine guns as they braced the militiamen. They were led to the road and ushered towards a waiting truck, the rear door propped open to receive the captives. Carl led the way, hopping up into the truck, the frightened Henrik right behind him as his teammates brought up the rear.

Just as Henrik pulled himself up, Carl pounced on the nearest Gestapo agent like a jungle cat, screaming at the kids to hit the dirt. He spun the man around in a rear waistlock before chopping him across the carotid artery, then using him as a shield as he reached around to take control of his submachine gun. He sprayed the Gestapo agents and the *Milice* with bullets, a couple of them returning fire and killing the human shield before Carl mowed them down.

"Load their weapons into the truck, and dump those bodies in the bushes," Carl ordered. "I think we can part ways at this point. Don't stop for anyone. If you get pulled over by the police or military, tell them you need to get in touch with Lt. Gunter Schweinberg with the SD in Berlin, that Carl Hansen sent you.

If you make it across the border, go to the nearest church and have them call your parents. Give the priests the line about our field trip from Bitburg."

"She's never seen anyone killed before," Henrik explained as Ingrid bent at the waist with her face in her hands. "She was in the rear with the supply lines, distributing medication."

"Hopefully she'll never see it again," Carl grunted.

The teens did as Carl ordered before gathering around him to bid farewell. They entreated him to come with them but he told them of his plans to rejoin his true love. They finally shook his hand, Ingrid kissing him on the cheek before they climbed into the truck and drove off. Carl watched until they disappeared from sight before slipping back into the treeline.

Harry Blackburn and Henry Geronimo had one last affair to attend.

The Dagineau chateau was cordoned off that night by groups of armed men in trucks bearing placards protesting the wages and hours provided by the owner of the vineyard. The city of Montauban was plagued by random acts of vandalism as city property was set afire and incendiaries detonated across the town. The resources of the local police were being exhausted by the activity, and they were unable to investigate the hooliganism around the chateau even if they wanted to.

Blackburn and Geronimo rode with Commander Staunton out to the chateau, permitted entry in a long line of limousines processed through the various checkpoints provided by the demonstrators. They drove up the winding road leading to the prestigious manor, where a great fleet of cars were parked so that their occupants could attend the great banquet celebrating the impending liberation of France by the Allies.

"From the time of Charlemagne to the time of Napoleon, never have our people been tested by the fire that we have endured in this world war. We have suffered greatly, but we have endured. We thank our Allies for bringing us this blessed victory, and we thank the Resistance for the sacrifice and the determination to lead us to this day. But most of all we thank our Heavenly Father for delivering us from evil and upholding our race and our nation. *Vive la France!*"

Angelique's speech brought the tremendous gathering at the Dagineau mansion in Toulouse to its feet in a rousing ovation. She stood at the rail on the upper level of the marbled staircase that descended as a horseshoe to the great parlor where everyone had gathered. She was resplendent in a flowing white silk gown and a modest diamond tiara, appearing angelic beneath the dazzling crystal chandelier illuminating the grand room. Beside her, the chief of police, the mayor, and her father beamed with pride.

When she first stepped forth and began her speech, a stunned silence fell across the parlor. The assembly was astonished as they realized they were hearing the voice of Madame Dominique. Her father had no inkling of who the voice belonged to as he had dared not listen to underground radio due to constant Gestapo surveillance. When he was told of what she had done, he was overwrought with emotion and had to retire from the party for a short time.

"Looks like I win the bet," Geronimo chirped as he, Blackburn and Staunton stood in their tuxedos, sipping champagne in a corner of the parlor hall. "Can't see her legs, but that face launched a thousand ships onto the coast of Normandy."

"Sorry, old bean," Blackburn disagreed. "We'll have to ask her to raise her dress before we leave, you won't take my money that easy."

"If either of you bastards go near her with such a request, I'll have you court-martialed if the frogs don't lynch you first," Staunton warned them.

"Hard to believe that someone coming into a pile of cash like him could be so tight," Geronimo quipped.

"Matter of principle, my boy," Blackburn toasted him.

Far above where they stood, Angie saw her father head for the bedroom chambers down the hall. The look on his face caused her great concern, and she eventually excused herself to inquire as to her father's condition. She started down the hall and was abruptly startled to see the door to her boudoir creak open, then close once again. She felt a thrill of fear which was quenched by her concern for her father. She approached the door cautiously before throwing it open and turning on the light.

"*Carl!*"

"I would've called, but I couldn't get to a phone," Carl smiled as she rushed into his arms. She was startled by his faint gasp, and drew back in alarm as she saw the blood seeping through the left side of his shirt.

"Oh my God!' she cried. "I'll get a doctor!"

"It's okay, no doctors," he insisted. "It's not that bad, you should see the other fellow."

He dropped back into a sitting position on her bed, and she immediately hugged his head against her bosom, weeping piteously. He patiently waited for her to release her emotions, finding himself greatly distressed by her turmoil.

Following his arrest outside Limoges, Jacques Tremblay was brought to a safe house along the countryside and debriefed by FFI agents before he was given a passport, identification papers, and one hundred thousand francs for his services to the Republic. Almost as an afterthought, the agents invited him to attend the celebration in Montauban before he left the country for Canada. Jacques purchased a tuxedo and made arrangements for transportation to the celebration.

He was as stunned as anyone else to hear the voice of Madame Dominique come from the lips of Angelique Dagineau, and he wandered about the ground floor lost in thought for a short time after her speech. He traipsed through the study, idly admiring the works of Gauguin, Renaud, Monet and Van Gogh, the promising young artists of the day. He realized he was coming into a new life, transcending the street existence that had once defined him. This woman had brought him into a new world, and the realization of what was happening was slowly dawning on him.

At once he had a compulsion to speak to her, to confront her one last time, face to face with no curtain or veil between them. He wanted to see her beauty up close, express his thanks for her intercession, and perhaps even kiss her hand. The thought of leaving this place, never to see her again without at least making an effort, was unimaginable.

He saw her retire from the upper landing towards the hallway leading to the upper chambers and decided to follow her. He could always ask for the restroom if questioned, and produce his papers if harassed. It was worth the effort, for one last meeting with the heroine who had changed his world. He made his way towards the steps and ascended with confidence, having left the streets of Limoges, and of Paris, far behind him.

Across the great hall, Chief Giroux of the Montauban Police had also come to celebrate the liberation of his country and give tribute to the patriots who made it happen. He ensured that his men did their utmost to foil attempts by the Gestapo and the *Milice* to intrude upon the proceedings, and had a number of his off-duty officers in plainclothes among the groups of protestors surrounding the chateau. He also wore a tuxedo and greatly enjoyed the opportunity to rub elbows with the movers and shakers who had converged upon his fair city at such a historic time.

Giroux had moved to Montauban with his wife and child shortly before the outbreak of the war. He was crushed by the Nazi victory over France and the establishment of the Vichy government, yet, like Francois Dagineau, was steadfast in maintaining his position in hopes of mitigating the oppression of his people and being able to uphold the principles of law and order, truth and justice. He had suffered for five long years, enduring long enough to savor this victory in this most fabulous of scenarios.

The sight of Jacques Tremblay across the hall filled him with a sense of indignity and outrage. Tremblay was a perjurer, thief and murderer from the streets of Paris, well known to Giroux from his days as an inspector with the Paris Police before he accepted the position as Chief of Police in Montauban. He could not believe that such scum had found its way into such a festive occasion, and that Tremblay was stealthily making his way up the staircase to the upper chambers in Giroux's full view. Giroux made his way towards the steps, moving as nonchalantly as possible so as not to alarm the felon, yet determined not to lose sight of his progress.

At the other end of the chamber hall, Francois Dagineau had sufficiently recovered from his distraction to compose himself in returning to the festivities. He had retired to his room and nearly collapsed with emotion, sobbing terribly at the thought of his daughter having been in such peril without his slightest knowledge. At first he refused to believe that such a thing had transpired, that there had been a mistake, until the looks on the faces of all who had heard left no doubt in his mind whatsoever. He was then overwhelmed by a surge of rage in realizing how Angie had taken such a course of action without his advice or blessings. He thought of rushing down the hall and taking her aside to rebuke her for breaking his heart, only to reconsider his anger and come to a further realization that all that had happened was for the good of the people of France.

At that, he was filled with grief and began weeping again, until he checked himself and thought of how pathetic he seemed in light of his image as one of the pillars of Montauban society. His guests, he mused, would be shocked to see the depths to which he was falling. He wiped his eyes and composed himself, determined to maintain his composure when facing Angie, accepting what she had done as a daughter of France and, moreover, the heiress of the Dagineau chateau.

He strode along the hallway when, at once, he spotted Chief Giroux moving purposefully towards the staircase. He was well aware of the ways and manners of the police, having survived in a barely endurable existence alongside the Gestapo and its minions for five tortuous years. He knew Giroux was trying to remain inconspicuous, and he could only think of one thing. Apparently Giroux had learned of Angie's activity with the underground, and was taking it upon himself to investigate. He was sure that Giroux was beyond reproach, yet he had no idea what Angie's operations with the Resistance may have entailed. She might have been involved in illegal activity or perhaps had knowledge of a criminal incident. Regardless, he would protect his daughter with everything he had, and would not allow her to be questioned or confronted outside his presence.

Down the hall, in her bedroom, tears spilled down Angie's cheeks as she cut a pillowcase to shreds in changing Carl's bandages. Her knees buckled as she gazed in horror upon Carl's side, and she wept bitterly as she applied ointments to the terrific wound.

"You know, if I thought you were going to ruin your makeup like this, I would have waited until after the party."

"Carl, you're breaking my heart, how can you ask this of me!" she wailed. "There are at least a dozen doctors downstairs, any one of which would do anything for my father! How can you be so cruel as to force me to watch you die!"

"Darling, I'm not going anywhere," he managed. "I've seen men with neck wounds worse than this. Look, the regiment I was with has been charged with murder by the Allied forces. If I am captured you'll never see me again. If I can rest until morning we can make plans to cross into Spain. There are rebels in the Basque provinces who would welcome us there. We can get ourselves situated long enough to make plans for the future."

"Carl, I'm not a fool!" she grabbed his arms. "You won't live until morning!"

"Dominique," she heard a familiar voice outside the door.

"No!" she exclaimed. "Don't come in, I'll be out in a minute!"

"*You!*"

The door opened and closed to reveal Jacques Tremblay, who slipped into the room and stood transfixed at the sight of Carl Hansen lying on the bed behind her, grinning wolfishly at him.

"Looks like your Papa's inviting everyone and anyone these days," Carl smirked.

"Dominique," Jacques managed, "do you know who that is?"

"My name's not Dominique, it's Angelique Dagineau, my father owns this property," she composed herself. "This is my fiancée, he's badly wounded."

"No, wait," Jacques' temples began throbbing as the red lights danced before his eyes. "This piece of shit is a mass murderer. They hung a hundred people from the street lights in Tulle, I saw the bodies with my own eyes. His partner shot and killed my whole crew in a church just a couple of weeks ago. He nearly killed me with a grenade!"

"Well, it was the lesser of two evils," Carl said hoarsely, "a million francs' worth of poison as opposed to ten francs' worth of garbage."

"Carl, please," she looked at him.

"Don't tell me you're engaged to that killer," he demanded. "I know what I am. I'm from the streets, I've been a gangster since I was old enough to walk. I've done a lot of bad things, but I've never killed women and children! The Nazis, everyone knows they're butchers, but no one could imagine what I saw in Tulle!"

"Believe it or not, I saved your worthless life," Carl taunted him. "If I hadn't intervened, Captain Skullface wouldn't have let you leave that church alive."

"Please, please, this is too much!" she cried. "Jacques, please, for goodness sake, I'll come downstairs and meet you, I'll do anything you ask. Please help us, he's dying, he needs a doctor, in the name of heaven!"

"Not a move, Tremblay, you're under arrest!"

The door swung open as Chief Giroux burst into the room, jamming the barrel of his revolver into Jacques' back. He shoved Jacques against the dresser and frisked him, pulling a pistol from his cummerbund. He was about to reassure Angie when the sight of Carl stopped him cold.

"Only in France," Carl sighed.

"Mademoiselle Dagineau," he stammered. "That man, his tattoos. He is SS!"

"You know, I told the guys these tattoos would come back and bite us in the butt one day," Carl shook his head.

"Why are you arresting me, you fool?" Jacques fumed. "That fellow slaughtered six hundred people!"

"Shut up, you maggot!" Giroux slapped at his head. "Mademoiselle, it is clear that this cretin has coerced you to harbor his fellow murderer here!"

"Oh, why am I being tormented so!" she clenched her fists anxiously. "Sir, this is my fiancée, he's left the army to come home to me after five years, he's given up the fight, he's dying before my eyes, can't you leave us be!"

"Your fiancé?" Giroux could not believe his ears. "And what of this backstabbing pickpocket?"

"Sir, I personally enlisted his service to prevent the distribution of a million francs' worth of narcotics throughout the streets of Paris," Angie insisted. "He is worthy of praise, not to be chained and caged like a dog."

"I take it you never heard the whole story," Carl muttered.

"You have no idea who you're messing with," Jacques warned him. "I have diplomatic immunity. Weeks from now, I'll be assuming a position as an ambassador to Canada on behalf of Charles De Gaulle."

"Do you think we are idiots?" Giroux punched him. "Silence, you scum!"

"I'm sorry, Chief Giroux, but I'll have to ask for your weapon."

The four of them turned in amazement as Francois Dagineau stepped through the doorway, pointing a revolver at Giroux. Francois, in turn, saw the bloodstained sheets upon which Carl lay and was dumbstruck with wonder.

"Monsieur," Giroux muttered, "you are making a terrible mistake."

"I will do anything to protect my daughter," Francois was resolute.

"Papa," she pleaded. "Carl is dying!"

"How did he get here?" he squinted. "Who is this man?"

"They are both killers, Dagineau!" Giroux exclaimed. "This slime is an assassin for the Corsican Mob! That is one of the mass murderers from Oradour!"

"Monsieur," Jacques looked to him, hands remaining in fixed position atop the dresser, "I have my ID in my jacket pocket. I am an ambassador to Canada working for Charles De Gaulle. I came to invite your daughter to accompany me to Montreal on business as I assume my new post."

"That sinks it," Carl attempted to rise but was gingerly restrained by Angie.

"All right," Francois lowered his gun as Giroux holstered his. "We have a wounded man here and my daughter is terribly distraught. Downstairs we have over a hundred people celebrating the liberation of our people. Let us reason together."

"Carl, you can see that Monsieur Giroux is Chief of Police, he can help you, so can Jacques, and so can my father," Angie knelt beside him.

"How can you speak of this worm in the same breath as your father!" Giroux fumed. "This is an outrage!"

"I'm glad it's not your breath," Jacques stepped away from the dresser. "Okay, look, there's some people downstairs who connected me with powerful friends. Dominique—Angelique— knows these people. They can get that Nazi out of here. I just need to walk out of here without this guy trying to collar me."

"Purse snatcher!" Giroux snarled. "Gypsy!"

Jacques looked into Angie's eyes for the last time, seeing all he ever wanted in a life in which she was something he could not afford. She looked back with a sympathetic gaze that clarified all, leaving him the solace of knowing it could well have been another place, another time, but for the grace of God.

"I will order my men to clear the road," Giroux assured them as Jacques left the room. "I have a plainclothes man at every juncture. I can assure you that the Mademoiselle's intended will be transported as quickly as his vehicle permits."

"Thank you, thank you, Monsieur," tears of gratitude rolled down Angie's cheeks.

"Let me go downstairs and consult Dr. Beliveau," Francois insisted as Giroux left the room. "I am godfather to both his children, we went through twelve years of school together. He would never betray a confidence, regardless of how desperate the situation. Take heart, my darling, and you, Carl, he will set you so that the drive to the hospital will be safe and secure!"

"Carl, it will be just a short, short time!" she knelt beside him. "Everybody's working together to save you, we'll be out of here in minutes, my darling! Our whole future is straight ahead of us! We'll move to Spain until the end of the war, we'll be married and have children! We can go to America, we can go anywhere! Oh, Carl, our life is just beginning, my darling!"

"This is where I wanted to end up, my beloved," Carl wrapped his arms around her waist, pulling her close. "Just hold me."

He finally dropped into a sea of unconsciousness.

The Das Reich Division recaptured the town of Mortain and held it until the Allies nearly overwhelmed its position by enveloping the region of Falaise. They were eventually reinforced by the 9th SS Panzer Hohenstaufen Division, allowing them to break through and provide cover for retreating forces throughout the area.

The Allied attack, spearheaded by the tank divisions of General George S. Patton, forced the Nazis further East throughout the autumn and early winter of 1944. They retreated across the Seine River into Germany before maintaining a defensive posture behind the West Wall fortifications. Regrouping long enough to launch a counterattack through the Ardennes Forest, they reached the port of Antwerp by mid-December. They pushed forward to within thirty kilometers of the River Meuse but were stopped at Manhay on Christmas Day. The ferocity of the Allied counterattack nearly annihilated the Division, and they were forced back eastward to regroup.

The final offensive for the Division was launched in Hungary as they redeployed to break the siege of Budapest. They were stopped once more, being driven back to Dresden, from where they maneuvered into Prague but were forced back into Vienna. Once again facing annihilation at the hands of the Red Army, the remaining units retreated West and surrendered to the American Army in May of 1945.

General Heinz Lammerding returned to his native Dusseldorf and pursued a successful career as a civil engineer. On February 12, 1953, he was tried and sentenced to death in absentia for the massacres at Tulle and Oradour by the French Court in Bordeaux. The West German government refused to extradite him, and he died of cancer at the age of sixty-six in 1971.

Colonel Sylvester Stadler was transferred to the 9th SS Panzer Hohenstaufen Division, called upon to rescue his old Division at Falaise. His forces continued to fight alongside Das Reich until he was forced to surrender to the American Army in Austria in May of 1945. He died on August 23, 1995 at the age of 85 in Bavaria. Major Adolf Diekmann was killed in Normandy during the Allied invasion.

Lieutenant Heinz Barth had been condemned by the French government as the 'Murderer of Oradour-sur-Glane'. He, like General Lammerding, was sentenced to death in absentia by the Bordeaux Court. Living under an assumed name, he was arrested at his home in Gransee, East Germany on June 14, 1981 and sentenced to life imprisonment. During the trial, he confessed to shooting fifteen people at the Oradour barns. No witnesses testified to this event. Many felt the Communist government had coerced the confession. He was released in 1997 due to his age and poor health, and died on August 14, 2007 at the age of 86.

Carl Hansen and Angelique Dagineau relocated to Spain and were married in Barcelona, where Francois Dagineau hosted a grand wedding party and reception. After the war, in reciprocation for the Dagineaus' service to their country, the OSS managed to alter Carl's service records. He was reclassified as a special forces operative in the German Army, allowing for his records to remain confidential. He and Angie were granted visas to the United States of America, where they would accept teaching positions in New York City.

They were at the Paris International Airport the year after the Nazi surrender of 1946, preparing for their flight from Paris to New York to begin their new lives as Mr. and Mrs. Carl Hansen in their new apartment in Greenwich Village, just blocks from the campus at New York University. It was a balmy summer day in June and they were dressed casually, having checked their luggage and awaiting their flight when Carl was summoned to the ticket desk over the intercom. He brought Angie a hot dog and coffee before reporting at the desk, where he had received a personal phone call.

"Well, well. Isn't this a coincidence, both of us leaving Europe at the same time."

"Captain Ruess," Carl managed a smile. "How did you find me?"

"Our friends in ODESSA are miracle workers," Ruess chuckled. "Talk about a Freedom Train. Not all of us were fortunate enough to have fiancées positioned so well as to get our heads out of the noose. Congratulations on your marriage, by the way. I do apologize for not having been able to attend."

"No harm done," Carl replied. "So where are you off to?"

"South America. Not quite as exciting as New York City, but the weather is much warmer. There's quite a number of us coming over, hopefully we'll find it to be a home away from home."

"I wish you well, Captain."

"All the best, Carl. I'll keep in touch."

Ruess headed back towards the upper deck of the luxurious ocean cruiser, pausing to peer at his reflection in a nearby window. Inspired by the legendary French mime Marcel Marceau, he had applied a thick coating of white makeup and highlighted his eyes and lips with a dark cream. He wore a leotard swimsuit that accentuated his tiger-muscled build, and he was tanning well during his travels. He purveyed an intriguing figure that he could manipulate to his advantage.

He had himself declared killed in action and a spurious death certificate manufactured by ODESSA. He knew Magdalene would go on without him, she would find someone else. If she was to ever set eyes on the face behind the makeup, she would have ended the marriage herself, he was certain.

He returned to his recliner on deck where he sat between two lovely Argentinian women, a blonde and a brunette. They were part of the diplomatic entourage with which he traveled, no doubt provided for his amusement. Nonetheless, he would exploit his personal charm to the utmost to improve his position, not only with them but everyone else. He had to create a new future, beyond the Third Reich, beyond Germany.

"Ah, there you are, my friend! An early riser, I see!"

"Force of habit," Ruess replied in Spanish with a coarse German accent.

The newly-elected President of Argentina, Juan Peron, strolled across the deck and shook Ruess' hand as he rose to meet him. Peron was a handsome, debonair man with a strong personality and a captivating smile. He was resplendent in a white silk suit, and Ruess' companions were delighted by his attention as he kissed their hands in greeting.

"Pardon us, dears," Peron entreated them, "I would like to borrow the Captain for a short walk." They simpered in assent as the men walked away towards the Presidential cabin.

"I must say, I am really enjoying this Argentinian hospitality," Ruess grinned. "Those steaks at the banquet last night were the finest I've ever tasted."

"We pride ourselves on our steaks, not to mention our wine, women and song. Speaking of which, I see my better side has come out to enjoy this wonderful sea breeze."

Ruess was impressed by the beauty and majesty of the petite blonde woman who came across the deck to meet them. She had soulful eyes and a dazzling smile, the perfect complement to her regal husband.

"Captain Robert Ruess, this is my wife, the First Lady, Eva Peron."

"My pleasure," he kissed her hand. "Your reputation precedes you, yet you are so much more beautiful in person."

"You flatter me, Captain," she smiled sweetly. "I have heard so much of your gallantry during the war. And, I must say, I do like your makeup."

"And I yours, Madame," Ruess replied as they shared a hearty laugh.

"I had intended to attend the movie theatre before lunch, darling," she informed her husband. "I'll see you then, I do expect you to bring the Captain with you."

"Of course, my dear," he assured her. "Come, Captain, let us talk in my quarters."

They retired to Peron's cabin, an elegant suite resplendent with luxurious goldenrod carpeting, brass-worked fixtures, overstuffed furniture and exquisite works of art. They stood at the bar where Peron poured them drinks from a large pitcher of *pina colada*.

"My staff and I are greatly looking forward to working with you and your colleagues who are relocating to our country," Peron was enthusiastic. "As you know, although our Administration came to power due to a strong alliance of conservatives, industrialists and socialists alike, there are dissidents who seek to disrupt the natural order of things in pursuing their own interests. Our security forces are aggressively engaging these subversives, and I am sure that with your experience in these matters, this problem will be solved in a very short time."

"I've dedicated my life to wiping out Communists," Ruess replied. "I would consider this a sacred duty."

"In soccer terms, I would say that we are building a powerhouse All-Star team," Peron raised his glass to Ruess. "Colonel Adolf Eichmann is expected in Buenos Aires within the month. I have also received word from General Strossner in Paraguay that Dr. Josef Mengele from Auschwitz is arriving in his country shortly. The Angel of Death...and Captain Skullface. Who could ask for anything more?"

"No one calls me that," Ruess stared at him. "You'd regret it."

"I'm sure I will, Captain," Peron looked reflectively out the window facing the open sea. "I'm sure I will."

CPSIA information can be obtained
at www.ICGtesting.com
Printed in the USA
LVHW111149200421
684633LV00020B/94